It's Christmastime at Maitland Maternity, and sixteen-year-old Whitney Davis is pregnant and alone. What would she do without the Blakes?

Teacher **Diane Blake** has always worried about everyone else first, and taking in Whitney is her latest project. But photographer Jason Morris makes Diane see that catering to her *own* dreams is a real possibility!

Independent and successful **Suzanne,** Diane's sister, has no time for anything or anyone...especially single dads with kids. Then Diane finagles an introduction to Whitney's doctor, Doug McKay— and his irresistible triplet daughters....

Thomas Blake, Suzanne and Diane's brother, is unbeatable in the courtroom, but can't persuade Claire Goodman to marry him. Somehow he has to persuade Claire—and Whitney—that he and Claire are the best possible adoptive parents for Whitney's babies!

Tina Leonard is a bestselling author for Harlequin American Romance, with seventeen titles to her credit. At college, she secured a degree in fashion merchandising. Then, after writing for many years, she published her first romance novel with a British publishing house, their first American author. Tina is married to the man who beat her by one book in a reading contest in first grade—though he admits to having only turned the pages! Never one to let past setbacks get in her way, Tina is still happily married— and still happily writing. She, her husband and children call Texas home.

Judy Christenberry has been writing romances for fifteen years because she loves happy endings as much as her readers. In fact, Judy recently quit her job teaching French just so she could devote her time to writing. She spends her spare hours reading, watching her favorite sports teams and keeping track of her two daughters. Judy is a transplanted Texan, who now lives near Phoenix, Arizona.

Muriel Jensen is the award-winning author of over sixty books that tug at readers' hearts. She has won a Reviewer's Choice Award and a Career Achievement Award for Love and Laughter from *Romantic Times Magazine*, as well as a sales award from Waldenbooks. Muriel is best loved for her books about family, a subject she knows well, as she has three children and eight grandchildren. A native of Massachusetts, Muriel now lives with her husband in Oregon.

Muriel Jensen
Judy Christenberry
Tina Leonard

Maitland Maternity Christmas

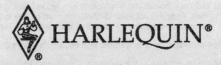

◆ **HARLEQUIN**®

TORONTO • NEW YORK • LONDON
AMSTERDAM • PARIS • SYDNEY • HAMBURG
STOCKHOLM • ATHENS • TOKYO • MILAN • MADRID
PRAGUE • WARSAW • BUDAPEST • AUCKLAND

Special thanks and acknowledgment are given to Muriel Jensen,
Judy Christenberry and Tina Leonard for their contributions to
MAITLAND MATERNITY CHRISTMAS

ISBN 0-373-83474-8

MAITLAND MATERNITY CHRISTMAS

CONTENTS

To Kimmie (Kim Kalberer Eickholz),
my beautiful little sissy. I still remember
Mom and Dad bringing you home
from the hospital. It's a joy to me that
my only daughter has grown up to want to
walk in your confident little cheerleading shoes.
You were a wonderful gift to me—and still are.

Love, Tina

ONCE IN A LIFETIME

Tina Leonard

Dear Reader,

I am very excited to be a part of this anthology, especially since I love family stories! I am blessed with an extended family—two half brothers and a half sister. In fact, this story reminded me very much of my little sister, who had flyaway hair and always walked on her toes! And now she has two tiny daughters of her own (with her flyaway hair). Lucky Aunt Tina!

In my contribution to this anthology, "Once in a Lifetime," Suzanne Blake isn't anxious to be cast in the role of mother again. But there's something special about Doug McKay and his girls—and the Christmas season—that sweeps Suzanne up. Doug isn't looking for a new mother for his children and Suzanne isn't looking for a husband. Can these two convince each other that getting together is a good idea?

It's such a joy to see the patterns of life—and family—repeat with little fingers and sweetly loving smiles. I hope you'll enjoy this romance of a man and a woman who embark on the special journey of love and happiness during the season that symbolizes the most magical gift of all—true love.

Tina Leonard

CHAPTER ONE

"ONCE IN EVERY person's lifetime, they hope to find their true love," Diane said to her sister, Suzanne, as they left the frosty December air outside to walk inside the Maitland Maternity Clinic. "No one wants to live their whole life and never meet their soul mate. Even you're not such a Scrooge that you'd deny that dream."

Suzanne watched Whitney sign in. The very pregnant teenager was due to give birth to twins any day now, and Diane had welcomed Whitney into her home until an aunt could take her in. "I'm not a Scrooge. All I said was that I felt like you push yourself too much, Diane. I'm worried about you." She cast concerned eyes on her sister. "You don't have to take everyone under your wing."

"It's not forever," Diane said cheerfully. "Today she needed a ride to the clinic, and you had a very nice car that did the trick most admirably. One might just as well say that you've taken Whitney, and her impending twins, under *your* wing.''

"I help people in my own way," Suzanne said quietly. "I don't mind giving Whitney a ride any time she needs one, but don't try to fit baby carriers into my car, Diane, figuratively speaking, of course. Since I sense that's where this conversation is heading.''

Her sister was only too aware of Suzanne's unwillingness to fit a man and-or children into her busy schedule. Whitney was a sweet girl, and privately, Suzanne was only too happy to help her in any way she could, but the trial balloon of practice motherhood she knew Diane was trying to float on her was doomed to be popped.

No matrimony, no children. She'd had her fill of motherhood when their mom died and she was left feeling responsible for both her siblings. Kids were cute—but freedom to create, freedom to do the things she wanted to do when she wanted to do them, was all this career-minded thirty-year-old woman needed—and desired.

"Oh, I'm not going to try to fit a baby

into your life, don't worry!'' Diane said blithely. ''Now, Christmas decorations, that's a whole other story. Look at all these wonderful ornaments on this tree, Suzanne.'' Diane gently touched a frosted glass angel hanging on the huge beribboned tree in the clinic's outer office. ''Someone here has the Christmas spirit.''

Suzanne rolled her eyes, knowing that Diane was making a second salient, yet silent point. Suzanne put all her efforts into the retail season, both creatively and time-wise. In her business, Christmas might be planned two years in advance. Department and specialty store buyers would order up to a year ahead of time. That meant her company's designs for scarves, costume jewelry and other accessories were planned and effected two years previous.

Then Suzanne spent the entire retail season, starting the weekend before Thanksgiving, in various chain department stores and specialty outlets assisting the buyers and sales managers in making certain the goods were effectively displayed, and filling merchandise holes where needed.

If her Christmas tree could be decorated

and displayed beginning January fifteenth a year ahead of schedule, that would be perfect.

This year's accessory in demand was the scarf she currently wore and designed. Its charitable theme—a portion of revenue would go to cancer research—and feminine colors were a hit among businesswomen, much the same way the preteen and teen crowd were devouring this year's assortment of overstuffed slippers. Suzanne felt so fortunate that she had designed the one item which was catching women's fancies on a mass level. It was almost as if with every purchase of her scarf, consumers validated her talent, and her vision for what women loved. She didn't want to think about the years that might come when she had the accessory item that flopped.

Shuddering, she said, "Diane, I'll just enjoy your decorations this year."

"Thanks. Whitney will probably feel less despondent with you there."

Suzanne nodded, settling herself into a chair near the tree's cheery, gold-flecked red skirt as Whitney was ushered into the doctor's office by a smiling nurse. "If those contractions Whitney is having are any indication, you may find those twins under the tree as well. You'll need an extra hand, so if you're asking, I'll definitely be there for Christmas morning.''

"You're a good sister," Diane said softly. "You're so capable and independent that Whitney says you give her courage for her own dreams."

Suzanne looked at her, caught by her sudden wistful tone. "Don't, Diane. Don't say that I've always been such a good surrogate mother or aunt, that I'd love having my own children. Tell me something. Has someone new, some really handsome man, come to work at the school? Someone you think I just have to meet?"

Diane laughed and settled herself into a chair next to her sister. "No. Maybe I'm just too filled with the holiday spirit."

"I'm being totally honest with you, Diane. My life is so full that I don't have the inclination or time for a man. Nor a pet. I don't even have time for Christmas."

"Well," a deep voice said from the doorway behind her which Whitney had walked through, "you'll just have to make time.

Christmas is for miracles. Who doesn't have time for a miracle?''

Suzanne turned her head to look up into the smiling face of an extraordinarily handsome man wearing a white doctor's jacket, a big grin, and a pink breast cancer ribbon on his stethoscope. Black hair sprinkled with gray, and blue eyes which showed mirth at her comment made Suzanne smile in return. "Well, you're a close match for Santa, but I see your name is Dr. McKay."

"I'm lacking the trademark belly, I hasten to point out." He reached to shake her hand, startling Suzanne because she wasn't expecting him to do more than make his observation and go on to do whatever he'd come into the waiting room to do. The doctor was extremely fit, but she decided not to agree out loud with his statement about his physique. "Doug McKay, believer in miracles."

"Suzanne Blake." She pulled back her hand and settled it in her lap. "Believer in same."

"Ah. I thought you were just espousing a theory more appropriate to Suzanne the Skeptic. Hello, Diane," he said, reaching out to give Diane a more-than-acquaintance handshake.

"How are you doing, Doug?"

"Fine. And so is Whitney. The contractions she's been having are mild Braxton-Hicks, a precursor of good things to come. You should have twins for Christmas, if I'm any proper judge of these things. I'm not often wrong," he said with a wry side look at Suzanne.

She rolled her eyes at his teasing manner. "I suppose confidence goes along with the graduation requirements in your field. No one would want an underconfident doctor."

"Unfortunately, the ones who should be my biggest champions are too young to do anything but squall their enthusiasm for my hard work as I bring them into the world." He checked his watch. "Well, back to work I go, but I've got a half-hour break penciled in after this appointment. Can I take you three ladies to a fast lunch beside the skating rink?"

Dismay flooded Suzanne. "Well, we—"

"We're free," Diane said enthusiastically. "Whitney would love to get out for lunch in a small, Christmas-decorated café!"

"You were saying, Suzanne?" Doug said with a raised eyebrow.

Suzanne swallowed, not about to cheat Diane or Whitney of a treat. "We're free, as Diane said."

He smiled. "Glad to hear it. Let me finish looking over Whitney's tests, and I'll meet you at the Rinkside Café."

Suzanne smiled, frozen to the spot. Diane said, "We'll be there!" her voice like silver tinsel ringing in Suzanne's ears.

As soon as Doug had gone behind the closed door, Suzanne whirled on her sister. "Doctors don't generally ask their patients out to lunch, do they?"

Diane shook her head. "I don't think so. He never asked me out, Whitney's his patient, and since you're neither patient nor previous acquaintance, it's a possibility Doug found you attractive."

Suzanne gasped.

Diane grinned at her, her eyes innocent, her smile self-satisfied.

A glimmer of awareness filtered into Suzanne, opening up a floodgate of realization. "You didn't need my car today! You dragged me here to meet him!"

"Nope." Diane grinned as Whitney returned to the waiting room.

"Admit it!" Suzanne admonished, ready to leave the waiting room upon receipt of acknowledgment.

"I didn't." But she smiled maddeningly.

"Diane! How could you!"

Her sister settled herself back into the chair and picked up a Christmas-themed magazine. "I deny all accusations of bachelor hunting for my beloved sister."

DR. DOUG MCKAY was used to making assessments—and the one that instantly came to mind when he'd met Suzanne Blake was *knockout. Sexy.* She had long dark hair that framed those wide chocolate eyes.

A little cynical, but not anything a doctor worth his degree couldn't mend...

From her caught-off-guard expression, Suzanne definitely hadn't seemed thrilled by his invitation. He could almost see her mind working as she scented out the danger, a hesitant woman who was possibly not as easygoing as her younger sister. Coming up with no good—or polite—reason to refuse him, she'd agreed to lunch, but not with a smile.

But dining was all he had in mind. Why not lunch with a beautiful woman? It was the Christmas season, and he was calling this fast lunch a gift to himself.

He'd read her reluctance, and that was okay by him. As an ob-gyn—and most particularly, a single parent of three—he liked to think he had an especially good seat in the movie theater of the female mind.

She'd relax once she realized she was in no danger from him.

THERE WAS NOTHING about Doug McKay that put Suzanne at ease. She couldn't help staring at him. He was kind to Whitney. He was interested when Diane told stories about her students. And without being overly solicitous, he inquired if Suzanne needed anything during the meal.

"Diane told me once that she had a sister who works a lot," Doug said. "I guess that sister would be you?"

Suzanne stiffened. "I do have a life outside of work."

Diane looked up from her salad. "No, you don't."

Suzanne glared at her. "I'm sure your hours are quite challenging, Doug."

"Yes, so I laugh when I get the chance," he teased.

She refused to rise to the bait, giving him a small smile instead. Doug was charming, and maybe she was crazy for not jumping on him, but the dating game would throw her whole, ordered life an edge she didn't want. Even if Doug was very enticing, she had no intention of being caught in a Christmas-trimmed trap.

"I like your scarf," Doug told her.

"Thank you." She raised her eyebrows at him. Diane had no doubt filled him in with the fact that she designed accessories for her company, so she wasn't going to acknowledge any warm glow inside her at his compliment. "I looked everywhere for one of those scarves for my mother. They sold out fast."

The glow she had tried to deny began to puff to life.

"My wife died of melanoma," he said, almost as if to himself. "The beauty of the scarf you designed is that not only is it lovely, but women everywhere can wear it and feel that they're helping their sisterhood. We speak of giving at Christmas, but so few people actually know how to give beyond their immediate circle of family and friends.''

Suzanne's jaw dropped. ''Thank you,'' she said, deeply surprised.

''Here's to a mind that creates beautifully.'' He lifted his glass of tea and nodded at her.

Suzanne could hardly draw breath. ''Thank you,'' she said quietly. ''I'm…very moved.''

He winked at her, completely neutralizing the numbness she felt.

Doug smiled at her for another second, before looking at Whitney. ''You're not eating much.''

''I haven't been hungry for the past couple of days, Dr. McKay.''

He looked back to Diane, his smile still in place. ''I hope you're ready for the big event. Twins are going to keep you very busy.''

"I'm as ready as I'll ever be. And Suzanne's going to help us."

He smiled approvingly at Suzanne. "So you do clear the calendar for some things."

Suzanne shifted uncomfortably in her chair. Was he asking if she'd clear her calendar for him? Maybe the comment was innocent. *He didn't actually say he was available,* she chided herself.

Letting her reserve slip just a bit, Suzanne said, "Well, I definitely want to be part of Diane's Christmas, and since it includes newborns, I'm bringing a camera."

Doug smiled at her. "You seem like the kind of woman who would like children and be good with them."

Diane glanced up in some alarm.

"I like children," Suzanne said. "I don't want any of my own, however." She looked at Whitney, who was staring at her with a pale face. "I'm going to enjoy Whitney's. And Diane's when she has a family of her own. But I'm not cut out to be a mother. It simply doesn't interest me."

He stared at her, and the look he gave her was somehow accepting, somehow wistful. "I understand," he said softly. He glanced at his watch. "You know what? I have appointments starting at one, so I have to get back."

Suzanne's eyes widened as she watched Doug get to his feet. He pulled money from his wallet, handing it to the waiter who appeared at the table. "Take good care of these ladies," he said to the waiter with a wink. "They're expecting twins."

The waiter nodded, putting the money in his pocket appreciatively. Doug shook Suzanne's hand as if she were simply another acquaintance, patted Whitney on the back, and squeezed Diane's shoulder. "Diane, if I don't see you and Whitney again before Christmas, I hope you enjoy the holiday break."

"We will. I've got baking and a million other things planned for us," Diane replied. "Thanks for inviting us, Doug. It's the perfect place for lunch."

He smiled, his gaze moving back to Suzanne for one last lingering glance. "It was nice to meet you."

"You, too."

Nodding, he left.

Suzanne turned to her sister. "Was it something I said?"

Diane shook her head, not looking at her. "His office is always busy, I'm sure. He had to get back."

"Yes, but he just…left all of a sudden!" Suzanne couldn't help feeling that she didn't know all of the story.

Diane shrugged. "Men. Who can figure them out?"

"You're not telling me something," Suzanne prodded.

"What's to tell? I don't know him all that well. He's Whitney's ob-gyn, and a teacher friend of mine goes to him as well. So I began taking Whitney to him on her high recommendation." She sighed, the sound kind of dreamy. "My gynecologist doesn't deliver babies. Her practice is more for older women with hormone therapy needs and the like." Then she looked at Suzanne with a mischievous glance. "Of course, meeting Doug is enough to make a gal think about switching doctors."

Suzanne straightened, her mouth dropping open even as she realized her sister wasn't serious.

"I could never take my clothes off for a doctor that good-looking!" Suzanne said. "It would involve serious toning up for a month at least before my appointment. And toenail polish. Even that might not be enough to get me into a gown and my feet up in stirrups. Actually, I'm positive that the women who frequent him must be very brave, and very secure."

"He's very gentle, and very understanding," Whitney said.

Both sisters stared at her.

Whitney shrugged. "Well, he is. And I don't think he's ever noticed my toenail polish. Guess you start to worry about things like that when you get older, though," she said, innocently returning to the peppermint ice cream the waiter had put in front of her.

"She's talking to you, Diane," Suzanne said quickly. "The *older* adjective was meant for you."

"Not me. I'm not considered older yet. Besides, you're the eldest sister. In some countries, it would be expected for you to marry before I could have a suitor."

"You'd be waiting a long time."

Diane laughed at her remark, but Suzanne

couldn't help thinking about what had made Doug disappear the way he had. One moment he'd been all charm; the next, almost regretfully distant.

And yet, why did it matter to her? It had only been lunch beside a noisy, white skating rink filled with colorfully dressed skaters with wreaths and gold balls hanging from the ceiling, and a feeling of Christmas in the air.

The magic of Christmas. Doug and Diane's talk of the phenomenon must have gotten to her in some form, because for just a moment, she'd found herself wishing Doug hadn't left as fast as he had.

She wondered if she'd ever see him again—and felt a little sad as she realized the answer was likely no.

Touching the pink-and-gilt scarf at her neck that he'd admired, a hesitant thought popped into her mind. He'd said he wanted one for his mother, but they were sold out everywhere.

What would it hurt to give in just a little? It had been a long time since she'd allowed herself even a date, dreading the complications that inevitably arose when a man wanted more time and commitment than she could give. Yet Doug hadn't seemed an overeager bachelor to her. No doubt he was still grieving....

And she was being silly. "I've got one sample of this scarf left. I think I'll give it to Doug since he wanted one for his mother's Christmas present."

Diane looked at her, as did Whitney.

Suzanne blinked. "What? What did I say?"

Diane and Whitney glanced at each other before Diane shook her head. "I'm surprised, is all."

"Why?" Suzanne asked wryly.

"Well, because you've made yourself go without a man for so long you've nearly turned into one of those mannequins you accessorize." She struck a silly, stiff-doll pose, with one hand out as if to ward off an approaching male, and Suzanne had to laugh, even if the truth stung the tiniest bit.

"I can't help it. Things get messy when I do try to date. I hate messes."

"I know. We all do. Doug will appreciate you doing that, I'm sure."

"I'll muster up my courage to go tomorrow."

Diane grinned at her. "I hope he's very appreciative."

"It's a scarf, Diane, not a marriage towel to bind our wrists together," Suzanne reminded her. But she wanted to see him again, and to discover if the attraction she'd felt today—in spite of herself—would be the same.

She was almost hoping the answer would be yes.

CHAPTER TWO

IN THE END, Suzanne merely left the gaily wrapped package with the middle-aged receptionist, who took it with a smile. "I can let Doug know you're here," she offered.

But the waiting room was full, and clearly the administrative staff was busy finding files and helping with insurance matters. Suzanne shook her head. "Thank you, but no. Perhaps some other time when the office isn't so hectic." She smiled and left, somehow relieved, and yet disappointed.

The receptionist handed the package to Doug's nurse. "Glenda, can you give this to the doctor?"

"Sure. What is it?"

"Don't know. But a real attractive lady just left it for him."

"Oh. Now *that's* interesting." Glenda's eyes glowed. "Was she a drug rep?"

"No. Don't think so. Seemed too shy for that."

"Hmm." Glenda walked back to Doug's office, where he was looking over some notes between seeing patients. "Package for you, Doctor."

"Thanks." He stretched out a hand without looking up.

She laid the holly-paper-wrapped box in his hand, and grinned when he glanced at it. "The receptionist said an attractive woman brought you a gift. You'll have to let me know when you open it, of course."

Doug was well used to his nurse's interest in his life. "A present?" He shook it beside his ear. "Smaller than a breadbasket, yet light as a feather...I guess Calvin Klein jockeys. A really racy pair, with mistletoe on them."

"Yeah, right." Glenda gestured. "Hurry. I've got your patients to prep, and I'm losing my own patience."

He smiled at the oft-repeated play on words. "No card?"

"What you see is what you got."

"Well, it's never too soon to open mystery Christmas gifts, I always say." He tore the paper, opening the box and sweeping the piece of gold tissue aside to reveal the scarf. A tingle of surprise went through him.

"Ew," Glenda said, peering into the box. "Suppose she got her gifts mixed up? I don't think that's going to look fashionable on you."

He smiled, replacing the box lid. "She didn't get her gifts mixed up. I wanted one of these for Mom."

"Oh, I see...."

"No, it's not that clear." He frowned, delighted with the gift and yet trying to figure out if there had been an invitation behind Suzanne Blake's generosity. "I suspect this is merely a kind gesture devoid of man-hunting intent. It's from a woman who doesn't want kids. Doesn't seem too fond of them. She's pretty, but she struck me as somewhat uptight. Uptight is not in my personality range, you know. I'd get on her nerves."

"Probably." Glenda patted him on the back. "Still, if she brought a scarf for your mom, clearly she's not too put off by your brood. Maybe you met her on her off day."

"We had a quick lunch yesterday, less

than thirty minutes. I didn't mention my children, since there seemed no reason to do so.''

''Women have been known to change their minds, sometimes as much as a few times a day.''

''She seemed fairly set on this issue. So there didn't seem to be a reason to pursue an actual date. Not that I was looking for one, I guess. So I don't know why I was disappointed.''

Glenda patted him on the back, like a mother patting a son. ''Because you're a romantic at heart.''

''Maybe. It isn't going to be as easy as it was with Martha,'' he said softly, his wife's name only a breath in the room. ''We just clicked. We wanted the same things, we enjoyed the same things. Women today seem so…so businesslike. So unromantic. I overheard Suzanne tell her sister that she doesn't have time for Christmas! Try telling that to three little girls.'' He shook his head. ''No, I'll write Suzanne a thank-you note. I'm sure that's appropriate, under the circumstances.'' Shaking the box one last time as he turned it over, he looked up at Glenda. "You did say there was no card?"

"No card. I believe she had hoped to see you, and then realized the waiting room was full."

"That reminds me. Let's get to our patients."

Glenda glanced over her shoulder at him as he put the box into a desk drawer before following her. "Could be you misunderstood her. She didn't realize what you were measuring her for, you know."

He shook his head. "Trust me, this woman was beautiful, and she was nice, but she didn't like kids or have time for holidays. Therefore, two of the a-b-c building blocks for success-with-Doug were missing."

"What's the third building block?" Glenda asked as they paused by a hallway sink.

"It's either easy camaraderie or great sex, and I'm not sure which I value most right now."

"Did she say she didn't like easy camaraderie or great sex?"

"Didn't ask." He scrubbed his hands.

"Did you go by this three-building-blocks theory when you went out with the other women?"

He sighed. "Debbie had Christmas spirit. Enormous Christmas spirit. On our second date, she mentioned that finding a diamond in her stocking would put her in the Christmas spirit, but that didn't seem like the kind of spirited fun I was looking for. Now, Christie liked my kids—or so I had thought. On our third date, in a romantic Italian restaurant, she thoughtfully told me she'd looked up a girls' boarding school in Dallas where the girls could get a great education and still be somewhat close to home. I was taken aback. That's not quite the mothering touch my family needs. Christie was a great kisser, but there's got to be more to a woman than a great set of lips. So you see why I'm torn between the easy camaraderie or great sex issue. I haven't been getting either."

Glenda preceded him into the examining room where the patient waited.

For a man who really wanted the companionship of a good woman it almost seemed ironic that there wasn't one out there for him. His three-building-blocks approach might be too difficult—and yet, how else was a solid relationship built but on common ground?

"How are you, Mrs. Mcafly?"

"I'm fine, Doctor McKay. And yourself?"

"Doing pretty well. Any concerns you want to mention during this routine exam?"

"No." She beamed at him. "I took your advice, though, and cut back on my smoking."

He snapped her folder closed to stare at her. "Did you really?"

She grinned, her advanced-fifty years melting from her face. "I'm down to a cigarette after meals only. And even that might be about history, as a Christmas gift to myself."

"I am so proud of you! How did you do it?"

"Thought about what you said, about being healthy for my grandkids. Decided it was time to see if I could—so I took the grandkids for a week and sent my son and his wife on a trip to the Mediterranean."

"Minding four grandkids for a week

helped you quit smoking?'' Glenda asked
incredulously.

"Have to set a good example. And, as
Doctor McKay said, they are the reasons
Earl and I want to be healthy. He's quitting,
too."

Doug sat on the round swivel stool.
"Well, I couldn't be happier, Doris. That's
quite a Christmas gift to me, too, you know.
I won't have to worry about you as much
now."

She winked at him. "I overheard the conversation you were having in the hallway."

Doug looked askance at her. "Oh?"

"I vote for great sex."

He laughed. "I'll keep that in mind."

"It leads to easy camaraderie later, as
long as you've given the relationship time to
ripen enough for the sex to get good."

"Great sex is not an option yet," he said.
"You have four grandkids and two children,
Mrs. Mcafly. What do you think about a
woman who has no spirit for fun and who
doesn't like kids?"

"I think that if you liked her enough, you
could convince her differently. You got me

to quit smoking, you know, and I never thought I'd do that.''

''More food for thought. Thanks.'' He patted her hand, then pushed the thought of Suzanne and her considerate gift out of his mind.

''YOU'RE WATCHING the door every second,'' Jimmy Johnston complained, ''and jumping when the phone rings as if there are springs in your seat.''

Suzanne blushed. ''I didn't realize I was. Sorry.''

Her assistant smiled at her. ''Is there someone special I should be screening calls for?''

''No.''

''Come on, you can tell your buddy Jimmy.''

''How do you know I'm not simply waiting for an order, or a delivery of material I want?''

''Because you're dressed to kill, Suzanne. You always look good, but today—'' He kissed his fingers into the air. *''Bellissima.''*

''Thanks. I think.'' He had seen through

her attention to detail today—she hadn't wanted to admit that she was dressing up for Doug, but it was obvious she was. Then, like the chicken she was, she'd let her faint heart steer her from his office into her car.

"Tell Jimmy," her assistant coaxed.

Sighing, she said, "I met a man—briefly. And I dropped something off at his office today. I didn't get to see him, so I over-dressed for nothing. I don't even know why I dressed up."

Jimmy raised a brow at Suzanne's red wool skirt and jacket, and the pretty pat-terned blouse beneath. "So the extrahigh heels are for my benefit?"

She had to smile at that. "Don't ask to borrow them. They pinch."

He grimaced. "I'd say that you may not think you like this man, but something caused you to don the red and heels. I gotta meet the man who could make you bring out the high heels."

"Jimmy!"

Shaking his head, he said, "I've been working for you for three years. Never have I seen you this dolled up. You're always professional, but today, you're beautiful. Really, Suzanne.''

She rolled her eyes at him. ''Thanks. Now answer the phone.''

He turned, snatching up the phone which was on the second ring. ''Blake Accessories. How may I help you?''

Listening, he turned at his desk so that Suzanne could see his face. ''Suzanne Blake? May I ask who's calling? Doug McKay. Mr. McKay, may I take a message? Suzanne is—''

She waved her hand madly.

''Oh, wait, she just returned, Mr. McKay. I'll transfer the call. Thank you.''

Putting the call on hold, he turned to look at Suzanne. ''He sounds nice.''

''It's a fabric rep,'' Suzanne said, gesturing to him to hurry with the transfer.

''My eye it is,'' Jimmy said, sniffing. He put the line on her phone, coming to hover in the doorway as Suzanne answered.

''Hello?'' She pointed to Jimmy to close the door, and he did after pretending to walk through it on high heels. ''Hi, Doug,'' she said, as calmly as possibly, though her heart was beating faster than normal.

"Thank you for the scarf, Suzanne. I appreciate it, and Mom will love it."

"You're welcome." And then she went blank. Couldn't think of one sensible, charming or even stupid thing to say.

He cleared his throat. "I'd like to take you to dinner as a way to say thanks. Would you care to join me?"

"Yes," she said immediately, the only word she wanted to say coming easily to her. "That would be nice."

"Tonight?"

"Sounds good to me."

"I'll pick you up at six, if that's all right."

"If you can, pick me up here, it's closer to your office." She was already dressed, after all.

"I have to make it an early dinner because—"

"That's fine," she said. "I'm dressed for just about anywhere."

"I'll see you then."

"I'm looking forward to it," she said, meaning it.

They said goodbye and hung up, and Jimmy nearly fell inside the door. "I can't believe you have a date," he told Suzanne. "A real date."

"It's not really a date," she demurred.

"Well, a fact-finding mission, then."

"That sounds horrible!" But she laughed. "Maybe that's what it is. I only just met Doug, so I don't know anything about him. Nor does he know anything about me. So it is a fact-finding mission, I guess."

"The wonder of it is that you're letting someone find out some facts about you." Jimmy winked and returned to his desk.

Well, it wasn't really a wonder, Suzanne told herself. There was no reason to date every single man she met just to stay in the singles game. She wouldn't enjoy it, because her heart wouldn't be in it. This was the first time she'd felt curious about a man. Curious, and attracted, and maybe even slightly hopeful.

And suddenly *very* nervous.

WHEN DOUG CAME INTO Blake Accessories to pick her up, Jimmy raised his brow at Suzanne. "I'll let you lock up. Good night, Doug. It was nice to meet you."

He left her alone with a very handsome

man. Doug was virile, tall, sexy, things her subconscious had noted yesterday even while she was trying so hard not to notice.

"You look very nice," he said, and Suzanne felt a trembling in her body.

"You do, too." *Now what? Jump into the car, have dinner, then go home, and call it a date? Is that the best I can do?*

"I couldn't accept the scarf without taking you out to dinner to thank you," Doug said, and she relaxed instantly. Oh. It wasn't so much a fact-finding opportunity for him than it was a thank-you between acquaintances. *Nothing to get overly ruffled about.*

She swept her gaze along his dark tweed sport coat, wool trousers and black shoes, thinking that sooner or later, she could edge her way up to looking at his lips without his guessing that's what she was wondering about.

When had she become so ill at ease with the opposite sex? "You didn't have to take me out," she murmured. "I wanted you to have a scarf for your mom."

"I'm thrilled with it."

She managed a smile. "I'm glad."

"But I've given you the wrong impression," he said, his eyes twinkling. "Taking you to dinner as a means of saying thank you is only one of my motivations. It was the best excuse I could think of to get a certain busy, no-nonsense lady to clear her calendar for me."

Looking at him wryly, she said, "As opposed to...?"

"As opposed to just simply saying, 'You're beautiful, and I'd love to spend an evening getting to know you better.'"

Uh-oh. The butterflies in her stomach returned. Fortunately, Doug spoke into the lapse of her conversation.

"We're going to Accordion's, and I must apologize in advance for having to cut the evening short."

It might be best, if she couldn't think of anything more exciting to say. "It's fine."

He helped her put her coat on, and the warmth of his fingers touching hers unexpectedly made her jump.

"Shall we go?"

Putting his hand out, he waited until Suzanne preceded him through the office door. She locked up, and they walked briskly to his car. After helping her in, Doug walked around to the driver's side and got in.

She glanced at him as he turned the car on and switched the heater up a notch. What should she say? What topic held common ground for both of them? "So, you've met my sister, Diane, and I've got a brother, Tom. Do you have brothers and sisters?"

"One long-lost brother." Doug laughed. "Actually, he's kind of independent, so I shouldn't call him long-lost. He saw no need to tie himself down to med school, or much of anything for that matter."

"A free spirit?"

"Very much. Right now, he's climbing Mount Everest."

Suzanne shivered. "That's not for me. I like sunshine and warm beaches."

"Me, too. Although skiing's great every once in a while."

"Yes, but there's always the cozy cabin or condo to return to, and other comforts."

"I agree."

A light rain began to fall, and Suzanne found herself comforted by the even swishing of the windshield wipers and the warmth of the taupe Jaguar. The radio was turned to a soft jazz station, currently playing a slow, mellow rendition of a love song. Suzanne found herself relaxing until Doug's voice broke the silence.

"Uh-oh. My pager." He unclipped it from his waist where it had been hidden under his sport coat, looking at the message as he braked the car at a stop sign.

"Duty calls?" She laughed lightly.

He shook his head slowly, looking off into the distance as he seemed to be thinking through something. "It wasn't in my plans, but would you mind terribly if we made an unscheduled stop at my house?"

"Certainly not," Suzanne said, so comfortably lulled that this minor bump in the evening was nothing.

"Thank you. There's a small matter I must attend to."

They made small talk until they reached his home, a large, Tudor-style residence. Rain splashed on the slate-colored brick stones paving the circular driveway as he pulled up. Suzanne noticed that as they approached the house, Doug became quieter, but clearly he had something important on his mind. She didn't wait for him to come around to get her out of the car, not wanting him to get any more wet than necessary.

"Careful on the steps," he said, taking her arm.

She was just about to smile up at him to thank him for his consideration of her when the massive front door swung open.

"Daddy!" three little girls chorused, rushing to hug Doug around the legs. "You're home!"

CHAPTER THREE

DOUG LAUGHED as he shooed his little girls inside. "Let's get Ms. Blake inside before the rain washes her away, okay, kids? And I'm only home long enough to see what you want. Then Suzanne and I are going out to dinner. All right?"

Three pairs of blue eyes stared up at Suzanne. She stared back, almost unable to get her breath. The children were dressed in mismatched sweats, and their short hair couldn't be called styled. They bore matching frowns of reluctance for her presence, which reminded Suzanne to try to recover her own smile.

The girls were not duped into returning it.

"Suzanne, I'd like you to meet Edie, Fran and Kimmie. They're four, and you may notice that I'm indulging their desire to be independent."

She glanced at him, her eyebrows lifted in question.

"They insist upon dressing themselves." He shrugged, clearly approving of their actions. "The look may not be what GapKids intended, but…"

Suzanne looked from him, to the children. "Hello, Edie, Fran and Kimmie," she said, hoping she'd matched the right name with the right girl.

They said nothing, merely clinging to their father's legs all the more intensely.

"Maybe not so independent tonight," he murmured. "Now, who was the smart one who sent a message to my pager? I feel certain Mrs. Hubert didn't send me an urgent note that said, "Daddy, come home now."

He smiled at a middle-aged woman who had been waiting for the greetings to finish before she stepped in to usher the girls into the kitchen. Suzanne had been so surprised she hadn't noticed her.

"Mrs. Hubert, this is Suzanne Blake. Suzanne, our family's daytime help and lifesaver, Maxine Hubert."

"It's nice to meet you, Suzanne," Mrs. Hubert said warmly. "My apologies, Dr.

McKay,'' Mrs. Hubert continued after she'd
shaken Suzanne's hand. ''I didn't realize the
girls had hit the speed dial to the answering
service while I was in the kitchen getting
their dinner. I am so sorry.'' She looked at
Suzanne, appropriately apologetic. ''The
girls are wonderful, but they do require a
constant eye.''

A constant eye. She was willing to bet
those words were a total understatement.

DOUG HAD SEEN many expressions on his
patients' faces: joy, sorrow, worry, despair,
hope. The only word for the expression on
Suzanne's face was…alarm.

Bringing her here was obviously a mistake. But the fact was, he'd felt bad about
not telling her immediately about the girls.
She'd mentioned not wanting children, and
he had accepted that warning sign, leaving
their lunch that day at once.

But then she'd brought the scarf, and he'd
admitted to himself that he wanted to see
Suzanne again. He had planned to tell her
over dinner, especially if he sensed the attraction he felt for her was returned. Honesty

was the only way to build anything between two people.

When his little imps had figured out a way to get a message through his answering service, he'd known they were in no danger.

But he'd realized that it was the perfect opportunity to check on them, and be upfront with Suzanne.

"Please have a seat here, Suzanne," Mrs. Hubert said, clearly more mindful of good manners than he was. She seated her in front of a gas-log fireplace, and Suzanne seemed to sink onto the sofa with relief.

He took an armchair beside the sofa, allowing the girls to pile into his lap to stare at Suzanne. "What's for dinner, anyway, girls?"

"Mrs. Hubert says we're having grilled cheese sandwiches," Fran told him. "And tomato soup."

Suzanne perked up like she'd finally found sure footing. "That's *my* favorite, too."

"Really?" he asked, certain she was only being polite.

"Absolutely. With lots of margarine on

the bread. And I put Parmesan on top of my soup.''

He thought about that for a moment, and the girls looked up at him, puzzled. ''Parmesan?''

Suzanne nodded. ''It's delicious.''

''It doesn't sound like it. But we should always try everything, right, girls?''

''Mmm-hmm.'' But they didn't look any more convinced than he was.

Suzanne lowered her gaze for a moment, then stared at the fire. He saw her sigh, though he couldn't hear it.

''Doug, is there a possibility that you could let Mrs. Hubert go for the evening?''

He blinked. ''Why?''

She shrugged. ''It's raining, and far more pleasant right here. I love grilled cheese, and am willing to bet that I have far more experience making them than she does.''

''Not possible.''

Suzanne smiled at him. ''Trust me on this.''

''I'd rather take you out to dinner. I promised you and—''

''Oh, Daddy!'' Edie cried. ''Stay home with us!''

He looked at the three hopeful faces staring up at him, back to Suzanne's rather more cautious one. "Are you absolutely certain? It doesn't seem very chivalrous."

"I'm positive." She slid off her coat and jacket, which Mrs. Hubert quickly retrieved to hang.

"Mrs. Hubert, would you like an earlier evening than you thought you were getting?" Doug asked.

"I must admit that the rain's got me worried," she said, looking at Suzanne with some unease. "The temperature's dropping, and they're calling for icing tonight, maybe even some light snow. It does have me a bit nervous."

"All right. You go on, and we'll make do on our own tonight."

"Thank you, Dr. McKay. It was nice to meet you, Suzanne."

"You, too." Suzanne managed a smile for the housekeeper, less stiff than the one she'd given the girls.

Well, Suzanne had a right to be shell-shocked. He would be if she'd sprung three kids on him. "What do you think about a glass of wine to go with that sandwich?"

"That would be lovely. Thank you."

"White or zinfandel?"

"Zinfandel, please."

Nodding, he headed to the bar.

Edie, Fran, and Kimmie remained on the sofa, checking Suzanne out. They huddled together, a slightly resentful, unsure cluster of big eyes and tangled blond mops. Reading their eyes, Suzanne realized that she wasn't the only one who had been taken by surprise. When the girls had paged their father, they clearly expected for him to return alone.

She couldn't blame them, as she had begun to enjoy having Doug to herself. It was time to break the ice. "When my sister was little, she used to like for me to brush her hair. Does anybody want me to brush their hair and maybe put some clips in it?"

Three solemn faces went side to side in the negative.

Suzanne cleared her throat. "I could tell you a story."

Silence.

She shouldn't be hesitant with children. Unconsciously, Suzanne frowned. She'd been a good substitute mother figure for

Tom and Diane; her siblings had many times mentioned that they'd been fortunate in everything she'd done for them.

Of course, the difference was that Tom and Diane had been older than these children, in their early teens. Her unofficial job had mainly been keeping the house together, maintaining schedules, getting food to the table—whatever she could to help Mrs. Dee, the housekeeper and cook, out as much as possible. She felt responsible for her younger siblings.

Doug returned, and gratefully Suzanne took the glass of wine he offered. "Shall we move to the kitchen? Are you hungry, Suzanne?"

She wasn't, but the light in the girls' eyes indicated that they were ready to eat sooner rather than later. "I'm ready if you are."

The girls needed no further prodding. They scrambled off the sofa and scurried from the room.

"If you survive tonight and still want to at another time, I insist upon taking you out to a nice restaurant. I promise you it wasn't my intention to pay back your kindness with tomato soup."

She smiled, feeling easier with the situation. "I didn't need to be repaid, Doug. And as a word of warning, I have been known to burn the occasional sandwich. You may get to spring for a delivery pizza if this doesn't go well."

He stood, grinning. "The pressure is on. Your audience awaits." He gestured to her to precede him from the room, and guided her down to the kitchen.

Edie, Fran and Kimmie were atop bar stools, elbows on the granite countertop where they had clear view of the stove. "I think I can handle the pressure," Suzanne murmured for Doug alone to hear. "Just watch me turn your hungry little crew into docile angels."

Picking up an apron Mrs. Hubert had left on the counter in her hurry to get a start on the approaching weather, Suzanne covered her skirt and blouse. Doug tied the apron behind her, his fingers sure at her back. Unexpected fluttering began in her blood all over again.

The girls watched, clearly anxious to see if Suzanne could produce decent fare.

"How can I assist you?" Doug asked.

"By getting out the soup, the skillet and pot you want me to use, and pouring whatever the girls want to drink. Think you can handle that, Doctor?"

He grinned at her. "I think so."

"Paper plates and bowls as well."

He lifted a brow. "Paper?"

"Would you rather wash dishes or watch any snowfall we might have with your daughters?"

The girls, listening to this exchange, rounded their eyes and quickly glanced out the bank of windows in the kitchen.

"Daddy, I have to use the bathroom," Edie piped up.

"So do I," Kimmie said.

"And that makes me think it would be worthwhile for all of us to take a bathroom break. Can you find your way around the kitchen while we wash up, Suzanne?"

"I believe so." She smiled at him, but inside, she was apprehensive.

She could grill a mean cheese sandwich, but the truth was, she was out of her league here. What did she know about young children?

The best thing to do would be to gracefully enjoy the evening—and then truthfully tell Doug that he wouldn't need to take her out to a fancy restaurant after all.

It wouldn't be fair to him. Because if she knew anything about herself, it was that she didn't want to be a mother figure again. These children would need a lot of time and attention. She needed silence to create, not distractions. Her job kept her busy even on holidays and weekends.

To become attached to Doug, and to his girls—or worse, to allow them to develop an attachment to her—wouldn't be fair to any of them.

DOUG ADMIRED the way Suzanne satisfied his young ladies' craving for grilled cheese sandwiches and tomato soup—even if he sensed her hesitance around them. "I should bathe you, but I'm letting you off the hook tonight," he told them. "One night surely can't make a difference."

Suzanne shook her head. "If we have snow by the time they awaken in the morning, they might need a bath after playing in it since they'll most likely get hot and sweaty in their heavy clothing."

"Oh, I doubt Mrs. Hubert will want them playing in the snow," he said quietly, as the girls stared out the window into the darkness. "She's a sweet soul, but not much for playing in the snow."

"Well, speaking of weather conditions, I'd better let you put your girls to bed and get home myself."

"Can I put them to bed and then talk you into a nightcap in front of the fireplace?"

She hesitated for a fraction of a second. "The offer is tempting, but if I don't go, you may end up with an extra houseguest if the roads get bad enough." She looked thoughtful for a moment, then removed her apron. "I'd better call a cab, as a matter of fact."

The phone rang, and he reached to get it. "Excuse me," he told Suzanne. "Hello?"

Listening for a few moments, he said, "I understand. Thank you for calling." He hung up and looked at the girls. "That was Mrs. Hubert, kids. She said the roads are already icing up around her neighborhood, and she isn't going to come tomorrow. You'll have to go to Grandma's."

"Yay!"

He grinned at their delighted shrieks.

"I'm fortunate Mom lives so close by. She can't keep them all the time, but she spells Mrs. Hubert whenever necessary. Anyway, if I take you over there tonight, girls, I can also take you home," he said, nodding to Suzanne.

"Oh, no, that's not necessary. Truly," she protested.

"I want to. This kills two birds with one stone, anyway. Excuse me while I call Mom."

The arrangements were swiftly made. Doug turned to Suzanne. "This time, we travel in the minivan. My wife liked it for hauling the girls and all their stuff around."

"Safer, I'm sure, on slick roads."

Suzanne went to get her jacket and coat. Doug watched as she left the room, realizing that despite the fact that she was being a very good sport, she was sending him no warm signals that indicated she wanted to see him again.

He admitted to a tiny sting of hurt, irrational though it might be, that Suzanne might be ruling him out as date-companion material because of his children. They were his life, all he had left from a marriage that had been very good for him, and for which he still grieved in a deep part of his heart. As much as he thought there was something magical that might blossom between him and Suzanne, he would never continue a relationship with a woman who wasn't going to feel comfortable with his girls.

Doug sighed. If it wasn't meant to be, it wasn't meant to be. As a doctor, he'd have to advise himself to accept the other person's limits—and move on.

FRANCINE MCKAY WAS delighted to see her grandchildren, and even more sincerely thrilled to meet Suzanne. "Come in, come in, all of you!" she exclaimed, ushering them into a warm parlor off the kitchen. "You must all be frozen."

Doug kissed his mother on the cheek. "The car was warm, Mom. Let me introduce Suzanne Blake to you. Suzanne, my mom, Francine."

Suzanne liked Francine on sight, and was charmed by her cozy cottage not fifteen minutes away from Doug's house. She could see many multicolored packages under a tall Christmas tree, no doubt most of which were for Fran, Edie and Kimmie. The ornaments on the tree appeared handmade—she suspected the work of the same grandchildren. It was clear that Francine adored the girls, and they'd quickly returned the affection before rushing to check for their names on the packages under the tree.

"Hot chocolate, Suzanne?" Francine asked.

Suzanne glanced at Doug, who appeared to wait for her answer to judge whether he needed to remove his coat or not. With a smile, he shrugged at her and went to unzip the girls' parkas, allowing Suzanne to make her own decision.

"The weather is bad enough, I know, so I shouldn't try to detain you," Francine said. "But I would love to spend a moment with you, Suzanne. It seems rude to send you off into the night without a cup of cocoa."

Suzanne smiled at her, captivated. "I can't refuse such a kind offer. I'd love some. Thank you."

Out of the corner of her eye, she caught Doug smiling at her approvingly. For some reason, his approval warmed her like the cup of cocoa Francine pressed into her hand.

"I'm sure I should be careful not to make some motherly gaffe," Francine said. "But Doug doesn't often bring anyone home to meet me."

Suzanne looked at Doug, feeling guilty. Except for the side trip to bring his daughters here, she would never have met Mrs. McKay. She was worried that perhaps Francine read more into her presence than was appropriate and might be getting her hopes up.

"I was just on my way to take Suzanne home, as a matter of fact," he said mildly. "Mrs. Hubert called as we were getting ready to call it a night."

"Oh. I see." Francine seemed to draw her own conclusion about that. "Well, now that I've got the girls, there's certainly no reason to cut your evening short," she said brightly.

"Suzanne has to work tomorrow, as do I." He stood. "Girls, let me help you brush your teeth so I can kiss you good-night and tuck you into bed."

"We can brush our teeth ourselves, Daddy," Edie assured him.

"We're celebrating Independence Day at Christmastime," he told his mom dryly.

"I thought I recognized that by the hairstyles. Goodness, girls, you're going to have to humor Grandma and let me brush that hair. Excuse me, Suzanne, but if you don't mind, I'm going to see what I can do with these wildflowers of Doug's. It was a pleasure to meet you."

Suzanne smiled at her. "Thank you, Francine. It was a pleasure to meet you as well."

"Well, come on, little wildflowers. In my day, I didn't go to bed until I'd brushed my hair a hundred strokes." Suzanne could hear her tell the girls this as they left the room.

"I'll be there to kiss you good-night in a minute," Doug called after them. Slowly, he turned to look at Suzanne.

"A little more than you bargained for tonight?"

"It's all right. I didn't mind."

A moment of silence passed between them. "I'd better go check on them and kiss the girls good-night. I'll be right back."

Suzanne nodded, watching as Doug walked from the parlor. He was tall, broadshouldered. Smart. Kind. Gentle.

Probably a woman's dream come true.

She regretted that it wasn't hers. The fact

was, Fran, Edie and Kimmie needed—and
deserved—a lot of time and attention which
she simply didn't have to give.

But they were cute, in their tousled, try-
ing-to-be-independent ways.

Idly, she picked up a pen from the
counter, and began to draw on a paper napkin three little girls holding hands. The girls
danced in a horizontal line, more stick figure
than real, emoting togetherness in their
dance. She interspersed hearts and wildflowers among them; a spring motif. "Mother's
Day," she murmured, the idea for a new design coming to life before her eyes.

"Feeling inspired?" Doug asked, his bar-
itone voice soft as he looked over her shoulder.

She jumped. She was used to silence
when she drew—and she never showed anyone her work until it was ready to go to
board, not even Jimmy, though he constantly
harassed her for a peek.

"Looks familiar." She could hear the
smile in Doug's voice. "Especially the
springy, wild hair."

"I'm sorry." Suzanne glanced at him.
"You're not offended?"

"No. I'm intrigued. My girls make me either want to reach for the aspirin bottle or a beer after I put them to bed. They tire a guy out!"

"I thought my life was hectic. You've got your hands full, Dr. McKay."

"It's better that way."

For just a moment, a shadow crossed his face. Suzanne moved her hand from where she'd been protecting her new sketch. Suddenly, she didn't feel quite as exposed by revealing her inspiration. "How long has your wife been gone, Doug?"

"Just over two years." His voice was soft. "The girls still want their mommy."

Suzanne looked at him, her heart touched.

"My doctor friends prescribe dating. But I always imagine that what they're doing is trying to get me back on the old horse. As if I'd lost my dog, a new puppy would replace the pain." He looked into her eyes, his emotions bare for her to see. "It just doesn't work that way."

She shook her head slowly. "No. It doesn't."

"There's no prescription to heal a broken heart." He sighed, long and deep. "Not that

I mean to be maudlin. I'm sorry. This was a lot to dump on you in one night.''

Their gazes met, held, lingered.

''We'd better go,'' Suzanne said, unsure of all the feelings beginning to seep through her.

''Yes. I've kept you out far too late.''

''Please give my thanks to your mom.''

''She'll feel more than your appreciation when she opens your scarf and realizes you designed it. That's an amazing gift to be able to give, Suzanne.'' He touched the napkin she'd drawn her design on. ''You have more to give me than I have to give you.''

''I—I don't know if that's true.'' Her hand covered his on the napkin for the slightest of seconds. ''We're just at different places in our lives, I think.''

He nodded. ''Maybe you're right. Let me get your coat.''

She heard him say good-night to his mother and promise to lock up. Bringing her coat with him, he helped her into it.

''Mom said to tell you goodbye. She's curled up with all three girls in her bed, and they are already asleep. She didn't want to disturb them, and hopes you understand.''

"I do." Suzanne smiled as they walked onto the porch. "It's getting colder."

Doug locked the door, pushing it to make certain the lock had been fully secured. "Yes. I guess that chance of snow might materialize."

They got into the minivan, and Suzanne gathered her coat tightly around her while the engine warmed. Jazz music filled the van, full and melodious now that the girls' chatter didn't override it, as it had on the way to Francine's.

She gave him directions to her apartment and before she knew it, they'd arrived. He pulled up in front of the covered entryway. "I'll walk you in."

"Not necessary, but thank you. It's totally secure in my building."

"It's necessary." Doug got out of the van and opened the door for Suzanne.

She stared up at him. "I did have a good time."

"Grilled cheese sandwiches, kids and all?" He smiled, uneasily. "I had a great time. You're a lovely lady."

Without hesitation, she reached up and kissed his cheek. "Good night," she said.

"Good night," he replied.

He didn't reach to detain her, so Suzanne made as graceful an exit as possible. Letting herself into her apartment, she waved at Doug through the window. He waved back, got into the van and drove away.

With a loud sigh, she collapsed into a chair by the window.

She just couldn't fall for Doug McKay. He was a loaded package, and she wasn't the one to open it.

Snatching up the phone, she dialed Diane. "Did you know Doug McKay has three children?"

"Yes. Their picture is up in the hallway of his office. So?"

"We went out tonight."

"Oh?" Interest perked in Diane's voice. "Is he awesome?"

"Yes, he is," Suzanne said. "He loved his wife, he loves his mom, he loves his kids, he's got a great practice. What's not awesome?"

"The fact that he's got three kids?" Diane asked.

"And doesn't that make me sound like

the Grinch about to tear the heart out of Whoville?''

Diane laughed. ''Relax. You're entitled to being gun-shy. It's first-date syndrome.''

''It is not! I wish you'd told me about his kids.''

''Why? It didn't need to be brought up by me.''

''You had to have known I was putting my foot in my mouth at lunch when I said I didn't want kids. No wonder he got up from the table like he'd eaten something bad!''

''Suzanne, you are you. It would be pretending not to be honest. He can't put you on a pedestal if he knows the truth. It leads to all kinds of problems when people aren't up-front.''

''I know.'' Suzanne's voice fell with her acceptance of that truth. ''I know you've got to be at school early tomorrow to teach. I'll talk to you then.''

''Good night,'' Diane said cheerfully. ''P.S., Suzanne, kids aren't the worst thing that could happen to you.''

''I know,'' Suzanne said glumly. ''But it's not the way I painted my future.''

"Guess you can't create your whole world sometimes. Good night," Diane repeated, hanging up with laughter in her voice.

Suzanne switched the portable phone off, staring out the window as big fat snowflakes began to fall outside her second-story window. It was beautiful, it was romantic, and she couldn't help thinking how overjoyed Doug's little girls would be when they awakened to a glistening landscape of snow.

Fran, Edie and Kimmie. With their flyaway hair, they embodied the word *flurry*.

Doug McKay's little flurries.

Reaching for her sketchpad and pencil, she drew several small flurries dancing on swirls of wind. Silver would be perfect for the swirls, and maybe the snow flurries. Almost as if her imagination drew itself, she wrote Love Is in the Air in airy scrolls under the swirls.

"Romantic. Illusive. Flurries of love," she brainstormed out loud. It was a pretty pattern, but one she wouldn't see replicated in her own life.

Fortunately, Doug's little flurries hadn't seemed any more inclined to drift down upon her heart than she had been to let them.

CHAPTER FOUR

"So, how was the date?" Glenda asked when Doug had settled himself behind his desk to look over the messages and notes she'd left him.

"The what? Oh." He waved last night's memories away from him. "Nothing special."

"The scarf lady didn't realize what a great guy you are?"

He smiled absently. "The scarf lady is wrapped up in herself."

"Oh, that's too bad."

Glenda left the room, and Doug hesitated as he waited for the computer to turn on. That wasn't a fair assessment of Suzanne, yet he'd wanted to stem Glenda's questioning. Suzanne wasn't really wrapped up in herself; she'd just been honest.

Which was more than he'd been, if he was to be fair. He'd sprung the girls on her, knowing how she felt. That would teach him not to be pushy.

"You big dummy," he said to himself. "You jumped the gun, and it backfired on you."

Suzanne had confidence enough to know what she wanted and didn't want out of life.

"I'm not looking to fall in love, you know," he told the loading Christmas tree and Santa Claus screensaver. "I don't want to get married again."

Santa dumped toys from his sleigh, and Doug watched, remembering how the girls had been so fascinated by the falling gifts when he'd shown them the screen saver. "But I can't just date a woman without knowing if she likes my girls. Even if we didn't fall in love with each other, I'm always on call to my kids. They're bound to run into my dates."

The gifts turned into stars, and Doug smiled. "I wish it were that easy," he murmured, "to give the stars to my daughters."

For a moment, he blinked back wistful tears.

"Dr. McKay, it's time to get started," Glenda said. "We've got a full house."

He watched as Santa reentered the screen, allowing another load of brightly wrapped presents to fall from his sleigh, exploding into beautiful stars. For some reason, it reminded him of the picture Suzanne had drawn on the napkin last night, of three dancing little girls, hair flying amidst flowers and hearts. "I'm coming, Glenda." Getting up from the desk, he followed her, pushing all thoughts of the scarf lady from his mind.

"HOW WAS the good doctor?" Jimmy asked when Suzanne made it to the office.

"He was fine. His kids were fine. Everything was fine," Suzanne said briskly, snatching up messages as she passed Jimmy's desk.

"Excuse me? Hold on, did you forget to mention kids to me yesterday?"

"Jimmy, I didn't know about them. It's no big deal. One date, a courtesy for something I'd given him. Don't make front page news out of it."

"So, where's the red skirt and heels?" he asked mischievously. "Since when do you wear jeans to the office?"

"Since it's snowing, and you and I may

close up shop by noon. Be glad for the jeans—they signal a paid half day for you.''

''A tantalizing ruse to get me to forget about asking how dinner was last night. Sorry. It's not going to work.''

Suzanne eyed her assistant over the mail she was riffling through. ''Jimmy, it was grilled cheese sandwiches and tomato soup.''

''Whoa. Big spender!''

She grimaced. ''Do you need a full day off, or do you have something constructive you should be doing?''

''I can take a hint.'' He turned back to his desk, a grin on his face.

Suzanne sat at her desk. There were orders she needed to put through and—

''You didn't do anything untoward to Dr. McKay last night, did you?'' Jimmy called.

She frowned at him. ''Short of smothering him with melted cheese and poisoning his tomato soup, I can't recollect anything. What kind of question is that, Jimmy?''

''His mother's calling, line one.''

''Honestly, Jimmy! Let's skip the drama, okay?''

"Snappy today aren't we?" He turned around.

"It's 'I'm considering skipping the employee Christmas bonus this year' spirit if an employee I know doesn't mind his own beeswax."

Jimmy shuffled some papers, not paying her threat any mind. Suzanne snatched up the phone and punched line one. "Hello, Francine. How are you?"

"I'm fine, thank you, dear. I thought I'd call you before the girls got out of bed. It's my only time to chitchat."

"I understand." Suzanne smiled.

"I enjoyed meeting you last night. I wish you could have stayed longer, but maybe next time."

Suzanne didn't acknowledge the well-meant comment.

"When Doug called last night to check on the girls, he mentioned you owned Blake Accessories. That's quite a coup—and a commitment, I should think."

Suzanne didn't have to think of a reply because Francine interrupted herself by coughing, and then sneezed. "Oh, my goodness. Pardon me, please."

"Bless you."

"Thank you. Now, you left a drawing over here that I found this morning, Suzanne. I didn't know if you needed it or not, and Doug's in surgery all day, so before I threw it out or lost it, I thought I'd better look up Blake Accessories and give you a call.

"I know sometimes people leave notes on cocktail napkins and the like, and it's helpful to have their inspiration in case they forget something later."

"You're very kind, Francine, but you can throw it away."

There was silence for a moment, broken only by a severe cough. Then Francine said, "You're certain? I don't mind mailing it to you. It's awfully pretty."

Suzanne heard the question in Doug's mother's voice and hated to disappoint her. What she really seemed to want to know was if there was a chance Suzanne and Doug might be seeing each other again. "I don't need it, Francine. But it's kind of you to call. You're not getting sick, are you?"

"No, no. At least I don't think so. Well,

I know you're busy so I'll let you go. You're sure you don't need this cute drawing?''

"I'm positive. But thank you ever so much, Francine."

"You're welcome. Goodbye, Suzanne."

"Goodbye."

She hung up, her emotions completely unsettled.

"No one's mother ever called me after I went out with their daughter. And I'm sure that's a good thing," Jimmy observed.

Suzanne ignored the comment, her mind otherwise occupied. Francine hadn't sounded as robust as she had last night, which worried Suzanne. If Francine was sick and trying to take care of the three "wildflowers" as she liked to call her granddaughters, and Doug was in surgery all day, that could make matters difficult for the kind woman.

"I can't help butting in a little. It seems like love is in the air, and I'm just trying to make certain you breathe it in."

"Jimmy." She gazed at him sternly. "Love is *not* in the air." But that made her remember the sketch of the flurries she'd drawn amidst swirls and scrolling letters that read Love Is in the Air.

Was she being Suzanne the Skeptic if she didn't want to believe that love could blow into her life on a Christmas-sent breeze? She'd skipped all things sentimental for so long she was almost afraid to allow those feelings to surface.

AT NOON, Suzanne glanced out the window at the falling snow. She noticed the streets were swiftly turning slushy, and that people were rushing by laden with shopping bags. "I haven't done any shopping, Jimmy." Nor any decorating, but then she never did.

Her gaze swept her outer office. If it wasn't for Jimmy's tabletop Christmas tree, there wouldn't be a single decoration in the office.

"I'm an excellent assistant, but I don't do personal Christmas shopping," Jimmy replied. He packed up a black leather pouch with some papers and put on his coat. "And I'm taking you up on your offer of a half day off before I get roped into your Christmas to-do list."

"I'd better, too." Suzanne got up, slipping on a thigh-length down jacket. "I can talk to sales managers at home just as well as from here."

They went out, locking up. Suzanne climbed into her white Explorer that had remained parked at work overnight, and waved goodbye to Jimmy. Staring at the busy streets of downtown, the matrons doing lunch and the holiday decorations on the light posts, Suzanne sat still long enough to take in the holiday scene.

Two little girls wearing outrageously striped, long ski caps walked by with their parents. The whole family was happy, laughing as the snow misted their heads.

She thought about Francine, who'd sounded under the weather. She thought about Fran, Edie and Kimmie. Their father was busy with work, their mother was gone, and because Francine was ill, they wouldn't get to enjoy the enchantment of the snowfall today.

And then, slowly, she turned her car toward the other side of town.

WHEN FRANCINE opened the door, Suzanne knew she was right to come and check in on her. "You are sick," she said without making an excuse as to her presence. "Do you have a fever?"

Francine's eyes were ringed by dark shadows, her cheeks flushed more than they'd been last night. "You know, I think I may have a touch of one. Would you like to come in?"

Fran, Edie and Kimmie stood behind their grandmother, their hair as wild as ever, and jam at the corners of their mouths. "Hello," Suzanne said to them.

They stared up at her quietly, almost sadly.

"Have you called Doug?" Suzanne asked.

"I haven't. I only started feeling odd a little while ago. Now I'm feeling muscle-achy and chilled."

It was clear she didn't feel well at all. "Why don't you go to bed? I can watch TV with the girls."

"I can't ask you to do that."

"What time does Doug usually get out of surgery?"

"Unless there's a complication or an unexpected delivery, I can usually expect him here by six.''

Suzanne nodded. ''Then do everyone a favor and go to bed. That's less than five and a half hours. I can handle the girls until he gets home.''

''I really can't ask you—''

''Yes, you can. You're going to get the girls sick unless you put yourself in a separate area. And then no one's going to get to enjoy all those presents under your tree because they'll all be too sick.''

That was the magical argument because Francine wasn't about to steal Christmas from her grandchildren, accidentally or otherwise. ''You're an angel, Suzanne. I believe I will lie down for just a while.''

''I'm not an angel. But I have some experience with kids, so rest easy on that score.''

''You have children?'' Francine asked, her curiosity not entirely dimmed by the flu-like symptoms.

''I have siblings I am close to. There were three of us, so I may have some insight into this little trio.''

Francine smiled wanly. ''I'm sure I'll be

better after a nap. Thank you, Suzanne. Doug should call as soon as he has a break in the OR, and you might just mention that I'm fine and there's no reason for him to be concerned. He'll worry when he discovers that you're here.''

"Go to sleep," Suzanne told her. "I'll tell him, and everything will be fine."

Francine disappeared down the hall to her room. Suzanne turned to face the three pairs of eyes gazing at her. ''First thing we're going to do is wash your hands and faces.'' If it's true, thought Suzanne, that most flus can be avoided by frequent handwashing, then I'll make sure theirs are extraclean.

They didn't argue, simply following her into the kitchen. After washing, Suzanne looked down at her small charges. ''Now, I'd like to play beauty salon. Who's got a hairbrush?''

Edie quickly retrieved their overnight bag, pointing to a hairbrush and box of colorful clips, never opened. ''Ah, the hidden treasure.'' Suzanne sat on the floor, looking at the girls with a smile. ''Who's first?''

To her surprise, all three wanted in her lap at the same time. ''Alphabetical order,'' she decided, hauling Edie in her lap. "Next Fran and then Kimmie. Then for our next project, we'll reverse order, just to keep things even. After that, the middle child goes first. It's a special and unique position," she said with a smile to Fran.

Thirty minutes later, tangles brushed out and clips set in the flyaway hair, Suzanne smiled at the threesome. "You look beautiful. So, who's hungry? I make great grilled cheese, as you know, as well as pb and j...."

IT WAS five o'clock by the time Doug finally got out of the operating room. Tired but pleased with his work, he scrubbed and changed, then called his mom.

She answered on the first ring, her voice raspy.

"Are you sick?" he asked, instantly worried.

"I think I might be just a touch out of sorts," Francine replied.

"Why didn't you call me? Are the girls behaving?"

"They're fine, just fine," Francine said. "Don't worry about them, honey, I've got Su—"

His eyes widened. "You sound horrible. Are you coughing? Is your throat sore? Do you have a fever?"

"Goodness, Doug. I'm fine. Truly. We'll all be here when you get home. Don't worry about us, because—"

He frowned. "I most certainly am worried! I'll be there as quick as I can. You should be resting."

"I've been resting. Honest."

"Not with my crew there, you haven't. Tell them I'm on the way, and to save their energy for me."

But when Doug got to his mother's, the first thing he saw was four figures lying on their backs in the snow, staring up at the twilight sky.

"Oh, for crying out loud," he said, getting out and slamming the door to his Jaguar. "You should be resting, you most certainly shouldn't be lying in the snow—"

Then he stopped, as Edie cried, "Look, Daddy! We're snow angels!"

He looked into Suzanne's eyes as she quickly sat up, her hair caked with snow, her red nose and cheeks slightly dewy with the cold moisture. "You sure are," he said. "The prettiest snow angels I ever saw."

DOUG CALLED IN a prescription for his mother after examining her, and then turned to face Suzanne who was now dry and warm as she and his girls sat in front of the gas-log fireplace. "I'm going to run to the drugstore to get the prescription. Does anyone feel like going with and grabbing some take-out?"

Edie, Fran and Kimmie jumped at the chance to go anywhere with their father. But Suzanne looked at him and shook her head. "I should be getting home."

"It's selfish of me, considering you've given up your afternoon to take care of my kids and my mother, but I'd love to talk you into reconsidering. It's almost no fun to eat Chinese food without someone to open the fortune cookies with. And we could pick up some sake."

"You have your girls," she said with a smile.

"Yes, but you and I can warm up the bottle of sake and share that, something my girls can't do with me."

"Mmm-hmm. Warm sake after rolling in the snow making snow angels? I don't think I can refuse that."

"Good. I'm happy. Okay, everybody in the van. Mom, we're going to pick up take-out and your prescription," he called down the hall. "Would you eat some wonton soup?"

"I'm never too sick to enjoy wonton soup," Francine called back.

He slipped into a zippered jacket, and together he and Suzanne put parkas on the girls. "Snug as bugs, you are," Doug said.

"I don't like bugs," Kimmie told him, her eyes big.

"I don't either, unless they're ladybugs, lightning bugs and butterflies, which are not exactly in the bad insect genus, I don't think, but never mind."

"What am I, Daddy?" Fran wanted to know.

"Well," he said, thoughtfully considering his daughters, "Edie is my lightning bug, because she lights up at night when she should be asleep." He kissed Edie's nose. "Fran's my ladybug, because of the three of you, she's most likely to use the hairbrush."

And he kissed the tip of Fran's nose. "Kimmie, you're my butterfly, because you're always flitting around trying to escape my net. Like now," he said, grabbing her and making her giggle as he kissed her nose. "But now I've caught all of you, so you have to get in the jar, which is really the van, and put your seat belts on."

"What is she?" Fran wanted to know, pointing at Suzanne.

To his surprise, Suzanne blushed a very becoming pink. He realized she wasn't comfortable being included in the family game. "Well," he said, getting to his feet to usher them all out to the van, "I think Ms. Blake isn't a bug. We probably shouldn't classify her as any type of insect after she was nice enough to come over and make snow angels with you, right?"

She blinked at him, and he couldn't read her expression. It had been so sweet of her to come over—and yet, he didn't want to read any more into the gesture than she'd meant. Suzanne was a nice lady—the kind who took pregnant teenagers to the clinic, who designed scarves with designated proceeds to women's causes, who made grilled cheese sandwiches instead of going to a fancy restaurant so the housekeeper wouldn't worry about driving in the snow, and who wouldn't let a sick elderly lady take care of three kids by herself.

Classifying her as a bug was something for which she probably wasn't ready.

CHAPTER FIVE

SUZANNE COULDN'T believe how much fun she was having on the ride to the pharmacy and then to grab the Chinese takeout. Doug and the girls sang off tune Christmas carols, and she found herself joining in. Once back in the driveway, they indulged in a very tame snowball fight, with tiny, lightly packed snowballs. Doug tackled her once— gently—and the girls piled on top as Suzanne scooted out from underneath, squealing with the excitement of the chase.

"Get off!" she huffed, having a blast and yet trying to sound like she wasn't as Doug grabbed the back of her jacket and slid snow under the collar. "Oh, my gosh, that's *cold!*" But she was laughing and he was, too, even as she pelted him in the face with a handful of snow and ran for the doorway.

She made it up the rock-salted steps before he grabbed her arm and tried hauling her back into the snow. But she had one last weapon left to her—a fraction of a snowball in her hand—which she deftly slid inside his shirtfront.

Jumping back to shake the snow out, he released her long enough for Suzanne to dart inside. She was sitting in front of the fireplace, her eyes twinkling with victory, by the time he'd ushered the girls onto the porch and removed their shoes to join her.

"Did you forget something?" she asked.

"Like what?"

"Maybe the prescription and the food?" Suzanne laughed at his oh-my-gosh expression.

Grumbling good-naturedly, he went back out. The girls came to sit beside Suzanne, less hesitant with her than they had been before.

"That was fun," Edie said. "I like snow."

Suzanne looked down at the three girls. "I had fun, too."

"Daddy's silly," Fran observed.

Suzanne had to smile at that. "I guess he is. It's probably a good thing for a daddy to be silly sometimes, don't you think?"

They nodded, giggling. Suzanne patted their knees, then said, "Sit right here while I go check on your grandma." Going down the hall, she softly called, "Francine?"

"Don't worry, I'm awake," Francine answered. "I couldn't have slept through all that racket if I'd wanted."

"Were you asleep? Are you feeling better?"

"No, I wasn't asleep, and no, I'm not feeling better, but after hearing my son laugh like that, I think I am now," Francine replied.

Oh. Suzanne's heart sank a little. She didn't want to get Francine's hopes up. Nor Doug's. And certainly not his little flurries. "Can I bring you your soup?" she asked softly, unable to think of an appropriate comment.

"It sure does sound good, not that I meant to have you waiting on me. Goodness, I should be waiting on you."

"Don't worry, Francine. You need to concentrate on yourself right now. I'll be right back."

She met Doug in the hallway. He towered over her, gazing down at her with an unmistakably masculine presence she found very attractive. In fact, she found a lot about Doug appealing. Enticing. Sexy. "Your mom thinks she could take some of that wonton soup," she said softly, gazing up at him. "Doug, I—I forgot a meeting I have early in the morning. Would you mind dreadfully if I...if I..."

"Are you about to make your excuses after all?"

She stared up at him, caught by the fact that he'd perceived her sudden panic attack.

"Don't, Suzanne," he said quietly. "I know what you're thinking, but you have nothing to fear from me. I completely understand your position, and have greatly appreciated your honesty. This is a difficult time for all of us," he said, stopping to swallow and take a deep breath, "because my wife died just before Christmas. So although it would be easy for us to get attached to you, the truth is, I know I'm at a vulnerable place in my life. I promise not to ask you for more than you can give."

She stared up at him, her heart beating hard. "Oh, Doug," she said, her voice soft. "I had no idea."

"I said I wasn't going to shortchange any-one's Christmas by dwelling on it, and I'm not. I decorate my offices like a mad Santa, and I'm going to overdo the holidays with wretched excess for the sake of my mother and my girls. I'm taking them skiing right after Christmas, where we can all hole up in a ski-in, ski-out condo and heal in the moun-tain air. But you," he said, sliding his thumb along her bottom lip, "you're not in danger of being swept up in our situation. I prom-ise."

Slowly, Suzanne nodded. "All right," she agreed. "Thank you for sharing your cir-cumstances with me. I won't feel so guilty now."

"Don't feel guilty at all. You're a surprise we hadn't counted on, and while we appre-ciate you, we know you're not ours for-ever." He smiled at her. "Now, if I don't feed everyone this food, it's going to be cold Chinese, and that won't go well with warm sake."

She followed him into the kitchen, slant-ing a glance at him as he prepared a bowl of soup for his mother and small plates for the girls. Diane would have a fit if she knew just how wonderful a man Doug was—no doubt she'd tell Suzanne how crazy she was to pass him up. *The eldest sister marries first in other countries....* That conversation came to mind, nearly making Suzanne smile. Diane wasn't averse to lightly applying guilt if necessary, but it wasn't going to work.

I want a husband some day, Suzanne told herself. *I want someone who won't mind my messy loft, someone who understands artistic moods, someone who isn't afraid of my success, someone who likes warm beaches and cold daiquiris.*

She glanced at Doug. *Or cozy ski resorts and warm sake.*

No way. She couldn't raise these three little girls. She was used to peace and quiet.

But rolling around in the snow throwing snowballs had been nice, too. She'd been surprised by the girls' eagerness to abandon themselves to the roughhousing.

It had been so much fun.

She broke open a fortune cookie, lost in her thoughts as she read the fortune. ''Little things soon become big things.''

Well, yes. That was exactly what she was afraid of. The teenage years. She looked at

Edie, Fran and Kimmie, remembering the threesome of her own family: Tom, Suzanne and Diane. She'd worked hard being the "mother" of their small family, even though Mrs. Dee took care of most things for all of them. But Suzanne felt responsible nonetheless.

Edie, Fran and Kimmie had a lot of family support.

They would do fine. It was all right to take Doug at his word and just relax.

AFTER THE GIRLS were tucked into bed, Suzanne sat in front of the fireplace with Doug, feeling warm from the sake, and the fire—and being with him.

"So, was Diane a hellion?" Doug asked.

"Was?" Suzanne raised her brows. "She still is."

He shook his head. "She's supposed to be an excellent teacher."

"She'll take on anyone's life at the expense of her own," Suzanne complained. "She does far too much, and not enough for herself."

"You could say the same about yourself."

"Well, but...I mean, this is all temporary," she said uncomfortably. "And then I'll be footloose again, and back to working like mad."

"What are you going to do with the drawing you did the other night?"

"Oh. That." She shrugged. "Maybe try to think it through the production stage, see if I can determine a market-driven idea for developing it."

He nodded. "Is that what you did with your scarf?"

"Yes. Although there's no predicting fads, I try to stay classic within fashion trends."

"You're sexy when you talk business."

She stared into his eyes. "Is that the sake talking?"

"No, but it's giving me a shot of bravery."

Her smile was wry. "I think you're brave, anyway."

"So you don't mind me telling you you're sexy? In spite of our previous understanding?"

"I don't think there's a woman on the planet who minds hearing that she's sexy."

His stare was long and appreciative. Suzanne could almost feel his gaze caress her cheeks, her lips. It was as if his fingers touched her skin in a way no one ever had. She knew he wanted to kiss her—and also knew he wouldn't do it unless she signaled to him that she welcomed his kiss.

Her heart hitched in her chest. "Doug," she murmured, "the way you're looking at me is…so patient. So understanding. It's almost as if I know what you're thinking."

He clasped her hands between his. "You probably do. Am I making you nervous?"

Slowly, she shook her head, never releasing his gaze. "Strangely, I don't feel nervous. All I feel is…happy."

His gaze held hers as he looked into her eyes, as if he were making certain that the answer she was giving verbally was the same one inside her soul. Then, as if he'd assured himself that it was, he bent his lips to hers, touching, seeking, hovering like a butterfly seeking a flower's sweetness.

Suzanne's heart stilled inside her as she closed her eyes, giving in to the magic. He smelled good, he felt warm against her mouth. She slid one hand up his chest, to slide around his neck, telling him that she wasn't going anywhere. The response was instant as he stroked her jaw with a big hand, kissing her more deeply, creating a bond between them that she didn't want to be released from.

I'm falling for him, she thought helplessly. *He's everything I could dream of in a man, and yet, I can't give him the very thing he needs most.*

"I DON'T GET IT," Jimmy said the next morning. "What's the problem?"

Suzanne shook her head, almost lost in her own thoughts as she sat at her desk. "There isn't one."

"And *that's* a problem."

"I couldn't explain this if I tried," Suzanne admitted. "Doug is awesome. I may never meet anyone else like him."

"You just don't see yourself slipping into a stepparent role." Jimmy shrugged. "Many women—and men—have grappled with that issue. Frankly, I'm happy that you're thinking this through. It would be easy for a woman in your position to fall like an overripe apple from a tree."

She narrowed her gaze on him suspiciously. "In my position?"

Jimmy put two blank art boards up on the easel in front of her desk. "Peering in on the age thirty psychoses. Biological clock ticking like a bomb. Scared of being left out of the two-by-two march through life. You know. All the stuff other women go through, except you."

"Jimmy, are you trying to make a point or irritate me?"

"Neither. Just glad to see you're not a victim of typical female worries."

"I see." She was too worried about the way she'd felt when Doug had kissed her last night to try to understand Jimmy's tangled point. When Doug had gently told her he understood what she was afraid of, and then kissed her so that she could almost feel their souls connecting, her whole inner woman awoke, singing.

Once in every person's lifetime, Diane had said, everyone hopes to meet their true love.

And now what? I specifically crossed children off my list many years ago. Those little girls deserve more than what I have to give.

I spend all my days creating, thinking, working. They deserve a mother who can...well, be the wonderful mother they need.

"They deserve more than I can give them," Suzanne murmured.

Jimmy shrugged. "Sure. Don't we all?"

She gave him a sharp look. "What does that mean?"

"That you're thinking of them as little baggages. Maybe Doug and his girls aren't baggages, but blessings."

"I know that, Jimmy. Blessings I'm not equipped to enjoy." A distraught lump began to rise in her throat. "Raising kids is a full-time job. They have emotional needs, even more in this case because they lost their mom."

"So did you," Jimmy said gently. "Suzanne, you have excellent survival skills you could teach them."

Her eyes wide, she just stared at him, speechless.

Of course, maybe it was true.

"And in the meantime," Jimmy said, "I believe they have much to offer you. In point of rebuttal, I submit these examples of your thriving creativity." With a flourish, he turned one of the white boards on the easel. A replication of her three-girls-dancing drawing was on the board, enlarged. "In your designs, you have always sought to nurture the female psyche. All of your work is geared not only to make a woman feel beautiful, but to give her emotions a lift, her soul a sense of sisterhood and beauty. Connection. Here, you illustrate that more beautifully than I believe you ever have. This is a gift, Suzanne, from you to women everywhere—but this time, your inspiration seems to have come from children." He looked at her closely. "A very surprising realization, considering your feelings on the subject."

She got up, walking to the drawing that Jimmy had interpreted on the board. "It's beautiful," she said softly. "Where did you find my sketches?"

"I borrowed them from your desk. I thought you needed a visual of what you have to offer."

He nodded, looking at the drawing. "You forged a new level here of satisfaction and pride a woman can have in herself."

"You caught it so well."

"It transposed well, because your vision was easy to see."

As if she waited for the next ghost of Christmas, she watched as Jimmy turned the board to another drawing.

"And if you try to convince yourself that one drawing was an accident, that you could never be struck by the same creative lightning, let me offer this as example B."

Jimmy's rendering of the love-is-in-the-air drawing was breathtaking. The full celebration of a woman's spirit was certainly represented as the soft lines undulated. Joy and happiness. "I see it," she said, her voice soft with admiration.

"I think most women will, too, Suzanne."

Their eyes met.

"But you have to allow yourself to embrace this new source of your magic. You have two choices. You can be afraid of this moment in your life, or you can embrace it and see where it takes you. I don't know if Doug McKay and his girls are right for you. But it does seem to be the contradiction of everything you try to provide to other women, if you deny yourself this unexpected gift.''

SUZANNE TOOK the boards home with her that night, surreptitiously, because she didn't want Jimmy to know that his words had affected her so deeply. She simply wanted some time alone with them, and her thoughts.

Propping them up on her dresser, she put on fluffy pajamas, made herself a cup of hot tea, and got into bed. A new project always excited her; it brought an extra thrill of discovery. Jimmy was right: Doug's children, and the joy of being with Doug, had inhabited her thoughts and brought her something beautiful to create.

She could wildly and freely embrace this moment—or she could let her misgivings guard her heart and keep it safe.

Having felt partially responsible for the well-being of her siblings, she well knew the value of playing safe.

CHAPTER SIX

DOUG KNEW the minute Suzanne drove away from his house that she had felt everything he had when they kissed. He also sensed her hesitation and eventual withdrawal. The kiss had surprised him probably as much as it did her. There was hidden passion smoldering behind their tentative exploration. He'd been shocked to feel all that he had.

He had dated since his wife died, without much enthusiasm and more in the vein of convincing himself he was still alive, somewhere beyond his grieving heart.

"You know," he said to a picture of Martha, in a silver frame beside his easy chair where her smile reminded him of how much happiness they'd shared, "you and I shared the same dreams."

He saw the joy in her eyes as she hugged the three girls. They were sitting on the steps on a warm summer day. The girls had been smaller then, and more dolled up than they dressed themselves now. Martha had loved putting dresses and ribbons on her daughters. "We wanted our girls to have everything. Friends. Parties. Ribbons in every color. College educations. Dance lessons. The only thing we weren't counting on was them not having you."

Tears sprang into his eyes. "*I* never counted on not having you."

He thought he saw sympathy in her smile. His heart contracted into a tight fist of sadness. "I've met a woman who is nothing like you, but she's wonderful, too. You would like her." His chest tightened painfully as he put the picture back on the shelf and sank back into the chair. "She would like you. You would know at once that the girls would be safe growing up with her as a shepherd of their well-being."

His eyes closed as he leaned his head back. "It's not that I'm looking to replace you," he said softly. "I'm not looking for a mother figure for the girls. I wasn't looking at all—and to find it when I least expected it takes me by surprise. The problem is, we're a package she doesn't want.''

Silence met his words. Of course, he hadn't expected an answer. The facts could not be changed. Christmas or not, he had to tell his heart that falling in love with Suzanne was not the right prescription—for her.

WHILE HE WAS ASLEEP, Doug dreamed of fairies that flew sitting on thermometers, and angels that sat in the cup of his stethoscope having a tea party. The angels were discussing how to make him feel better, and were especially interested in stitching up his broken heart. The human heart, as he well knew, was a sturdy muscle. But the heart inside his dream-body was made of fabric and filled with confetti. So, the fairies and angels busied themselves stitching the torn fabric and replacing the silver-and-gold confetti stuffing.

And when they were finished, he felt so much better that he knew he and the girls were going to be all right. The first thing he saw when he awoke was the picture of Martha, and she was still smiling, as if she somehow knew he was healed.

THREE DAYS LATER, a scratching at the back of Suzanne's throat brought her eyes open from a groggy sleep; at the same time she realized her throat was sore and her nose clogged.

"Argh," she groaned, rolling over to put her face into the pillow. That was worse, so she sat up, smashing the pillow into better support for her upright position.

Her reclining position brought the two art boards into view, which she'd never taken back to the office. Suzanne squinted at them, still not certain if she was comfortable with the new direction her creativity seemed to be taking. She'd never designed anything like these particular renderings before; Jimmy was right. It was as if she'd changed her focus without even realizing it, yet the change was fresh and inviting. This year's scarf had been a wonderful success; instinctively, she knew these designs would be, too. And the proceeds could be donated to the same breast cancer research fund she'd donated to this year. But she didn't want to do another scarf.

She just didn't know what else she could do. But these designs were special, she decided, eyeing them before snatching up a tissue and sneezing into it. "Argh," she repeated. Picking up the phone at her bedside, she called her office. Jimmy answered on the second ring.

"Jimmy, it's Suzanne."

"Sickly Suzanne, it sounds like."

"I am." She coughed, then said, "I'll be in the office in two hours."

"Please don't do that on my behalf. There's nothing here I can't take care of, and I don't want to catch your grunge if possible. It is Christmas, you know."

"I won't kiss you."

"Just having the germs around is more risk than I need. Thanks, but stay home."

She sighed. "Maybe I will. Call me if I get any important calls, or if—"

"Suzanne, the office has run without you on occasion," he interrupted. "You're gone more than you're in during the Christmas season anyway."

It was true. Vendor visits and luncheons,

as well as merchandising in various stores, ate up a great deal of her time during the biggest retail season of the year.

"Oops, gotta go, the other line is ringing. I'll check in with you later," he said, hanging up the phone.

"And that's that," she said to herself. "I'll just have to have a working day at home." Getting out her sketch pad and colored pencils, she began playing with colors for her new designs, all the while thinking of Edie, Fran and Kimmie's hair, the color of their eyes, and their laughter, without even realizing that she was finding inspiration where she'd least expected it.

AT NOON, Suzanne stopped working, giving her work a critical eye before getting up to go into the bathroom. She washed her face, brushed her teeth and pulled her hair up into a messy ponytail. Pulling on fuzzy slippers, she padded into the kitchen to make herself yet another cup of hot tea.

The knocking on the door startled her. It could be Jimmy, bringing her a delivery of material or a contract. Diane might stop by if she'd called the office and found out she was at home. "Who is it?"

"Doug," she heard, and as her heart leaped inside her, Suzanne realized that was the answer she'd least expected—and yet most wanted.

But she looked like heck. "What are you doing here?" she called through the door.

"Making a house call."

A reluctant smile came to her lips. "How did you know I was at home?"

"I called the office and Jimmy said you needed the services of a good physician. I decided I'd better stop by on my lunch break."

She rolled her eyes. "I can't let you in, Doctor."

"Why not? My services are cheap. And I brought wonton soup. My mother said it made her feel better."

"I don't want you to see me like this," Suzanne confessed, her tone reluctant yet laughing.

Silence met that confession. Then he said, "I could leave the soup outside the door."

She brightened. "Would you? I'm just vain enough to take you up on that offer."

"Sure. Why not? I'm leaving it now, I'm setting it down, can you hear the bag rustling? Okay, you can grab it if you open the door."

Smiling, she asked, "You're not really leaving it, are you?"

"I truly feel that it's in your best interests to let me examine you."

She really, really did not want him to see her without makeup on, with a runny nose, a raspy voice. But in the spirit of good sportswomanship, she opened the door. "Hello, Doctor."

He came in, setting a white sack on the counter. "I am the only doctor in the city who makes house calls with wonton soup." Coming close to her, he said, "Hm. I know what's wrong with you."

Her breath caught as he took her chin between his fingers, pretending to inspect her. "You do?"

"Yes. I've been thinking about it a lot, and I've made my diagnosis. You need someone to take care of you."

"For a cold?"

Steering her toward the sofa, he sat her down, then pulled her legs up so that she reclined. He put a sofa pillow under her head and a blanket over her. Retrieving the sack, he grabbed a spoon from the drawer and brought out a white foam cup of wonton soup. "I'm going to feed you."

"I can do it myself," she said, starting to sit up.

"Yes, yes, I know." Gently, he pushed her back into a reclining position. "You are independent, a thoroughly amazing goddess of a woman. But in thinking about you—" he sent her a glance "—and me and the girls I realized that you have a lot to offer us, and yet, we don't have much to offer you."

"That's not—"

"Shh," he said, placing a spoonful of broth against her lips so that she had to drink it. "And then I realized, you took care of your brother and sister, and you were very responsible. Now, you seem to think you'd be responsible for me and my girls. The thing is, that's not exactly what I want from you." He kissed her lips lightly, to illustrate his meaning.

"You're going to get sick," she protested.

"I'm a doctor. I'll get over it. What I'm trying to tell you is that you don't have to be responsible for us, Suzanne. I want to take care of you and hold you and walk with you." He put the soup down, and put one hand lightly against her cheek as he sat on the sofa beside her. "There's some things you'd be great for where my daughters are concerned, and yet, I'm not looking for a replacement mother. I'm not trying to shift my kids onto you."

"I never thought that," she protested. "I just—"

"You are a special woman, and I'd like to spend my every waking moment getting to know you better. And I'd like to spend my sleeping ones holding you in my arms."

"Oh, Doug." Her eyes filled with sentimental tears. "That's so sweet. I do care about you, and your girls. I just never—"

"I know. And I didn't, either." He fed her some more wonton soup, and she let him take care of her. "But I've never been one to look a miracle in the mouth. In my profession, I've learned to be grateful for the miracles I'm sent."

She stared up into his eyes, admiring his strength and compassion. "You're getting to me."

He smiled. "And it would be unfair of me to take advantage of a sickly woman. They say that sometimes patients fall in love with their doctor when healed by them."

"Oh, do they?" she asked, smiling. "Is that your prescription?"

"Actually, no. I want you to be completely sure when you think about me, and my girls, that I don't have you under any kind of hypnotic doctor spell." Once more, he lightly brushed her lips with his. "Call me when you're well, Suzanne. If you don't call me, I'll accept that your being with us was kindness on your part, to my mother and my family when we were having a rough period. We appreciate you, but we don't need you coming to our rescue. What I want is something more than that, and what I'm willing to give you is also something more than wonton soup."

He got up, his smile half on his face, and yet angled, too, as if he hated to leave her. "I'm going now, but think about what I said."

"I will," she answered. Watching him, her heart somehow felt as if it were leaving with him.

"My mother," he said, hesitating at the door, "decided that she wouldn't wait until Christmas to open her gift from me. She said that life was too short to wait, but I think she was looking for a pick-me-up after being ill. She said the scarf was enchanting, but when she discovered you'd designed it, she said that..." He choked up, his gaze leaving her for a split second. "She said that she'd fallen for Martha when she met her the first time, and that to her surprise, she'd felt the same way when she met you. And I said, 'Funny thing, I've been thinking that myself.'"

"Oh, Doug," Suzanne murmured.

"How could I fall for this Scroogelike woman who doesn't have Christmas spirit, and who doesn't want kids, I asked myself. But there's so much beauty in you, Suzanne, that my heart, well, my heart has healed in some miraculous way. You've done that for me. Physicians can heal themselves of many things, but the soul takes a different kind of wellness. Which is what I want to offer you, too. I don't think you've ever leaned on anyone, or ever let anyone take care of you, because you got used to being the one in charge. But I'm suggesting that what I can offer you is a two-way street. I've fallen in love with you when I never expected to, yet I know you weren't looking for love, either. I'll let you make the next move. So call me, if you decide that you need me, the way I want to be part of your life."

Then he closed the door. Suzanne's eyes widened. Doug had pared her worried emotions down to the core that concerned her most: he wasn't looking for her to only raise his family. What he'd said was what she needed most to hear.

He wanted her for her.

He was trying to give to her, yet she knew that he and his daughters already had given to her, in ways he couldn't possibly know about. She thought about the art boards with the happy, dancing girls and the swirling flurries and without further thought, she leaped from the sofa and raced to the door. Jerking it open, she was scooped right up into a hug in Doug's arms.

"God, I was hoping you would do that," he said hoarsely against her hair. "I was *praying* you'd do that."

She laughed as he kissed her lips, her

throat, her hair as he twirled her around in a circle. "And if I hadn't?"

Gently, he cradled her in his arms to carry her back inside the apartment. "Christmas is a time for miracles, and I just had to believe that you knew I'd fallen in love with you."

"I've fallen in love with you, too," she said, as he set her down on the sofa again. "And your girls," she added, thinking about the circle of joyful womanhood she'd sketched when she hadn't even realized her own life was beginning to blossom. "Thank you for your precious gift to me."

Melting into a kiss, they wrapped themselves in each other's arms, celebrating the unexpected and beautiful miracle of finding true love.

A HEARTBEAT AWAY

Judy Christenberry

Dear Reader,

Christmas is such a special time. Lots of hustle and bustle. However, those aren't the things that we remember, but rather the love and giving of Christmas.

It's been a tradition in our family to buy a special ornament each year, and as we decorate the tree, those ornaments of Christmases past bring back fond memories.

In my story, "A Heartbeat Away," Tom Blake has warm recollections of his family life, but his girlfriend, Claire Goodman, doesn't, and Tom helps her through that. She has to forgive herself before she can move forward.

Family doesn't necessarily have to mean biological family. In my family, adoption brought twin baby boys to my brother and his wife. So Claire and Tom's intention to adopt twins has wonderful memories for me.

I hope Christmas is a magical time for you. Reach out to create special memories with those around you. May the love and magic of Christmas touch you this year, as it does Claire and Tom.

Merry Christmas,

Judy Christenberry

CHAPTER ONE

CLAIRE GOODMAN leaned against the wall, squeezing her eyes shut, promising herself she could do this.

It would take a lot of courage. Heck! Who was she kidding? It would take a lot of acting. And she was lousy at acting.

"Claire! What are you doing here?"

Claire's eyes popped open and she found herself facing Diane Blake.

"I—I've come to see Tom," she muttered.

"Well, of course, you have, silly. I mean what are you doing out in the hall? Oh, you know Whitney Davis, don't you?" She nudged the pregnant teenager next to her.

Claire smiled at the young woman. She had a lot of sympathy for Whitney, a sixteen-year-old almost eight months pregnant with twins and trying to make up her mind about her future.

"Of course. Is everything all right?" she asked.

"Sure," Whitney said, looking at Diane, as if for confirmation. "Mr. Blake is taking care of everything."

Tom Blake, Diane's brother and Claire's...friend, was a family lawyer, handling estates, divorces, adoptions, anything that affected a family's life. Which was why she never connected him with his father, a well-known corporate lawyer with great influence and social power. Father and son did not travel in the same circles.

"Great. He's very good at what he does," she said, perfectly ready to praise him. That was her problem. She thought he was wonderful.

"Well," Diane said with a smile, "don't let us keep you. Go right on in. My brother would run us off if he thought we were delaying your arrival."

Claire's stomach began churning. "I'm sure you're wrong, Diane."

"And I'm sure I'm not. Come along, Whitney, we don't want to hold up true love." With a laugh and a wave, she led the teenager away, leaving Claire alone in the hall outside Tom's office.

True love? No, Diane was wrong. She was attracted to Tom. Who wouldn't be? He was charming, smart, warm, gregarious. Successful. What was not to love? His kisses were— Oh, lordy, she'd better stop.

Realizing if she didn't go in now and do what she had to do, she might never be able to. And she'd made up her mind. She was going to break up with Tom Blake!

TOM BLAKE CHECKED his Rolex again. It had been a gift from his father when he graduated from college, and it still kept perfect time. But Tom shook it, wondering if it could've slowed down. It showed only three minutes from the last time he'd looked.

He was too anxious to see Claire. She'd probably be frightened if she knew that. He was thirty-one, well-established as an attorney, from a good family. But he'd never met a woman who...completed him. Until Claire. He didn't want to waste any time. He was ready to marry her now.

Claire, however, seemed cautious. She'd particularly been thrown when she'd discovered his father was Hugh Blake. Tom chuckled. He'd learned early in life to avoid the people who pursued him to get to his father. And to avoid the people who showed interest in him because of his bank account. Particularly beautiful women.

When he'd met Claire, he hadn't mentioned his family. He'd told her what he did, saying he had a small law firm, and it was. He and a friend opened it four years ago. They were now the number one firm for family law in Austin with more business than they could handle.

Claire, a nurse at Maitland Maternity Clinic who specialized in caring for preemies, accepted him as her equal. They'd chatted, found many things in common, and he'd wanted to haul her off so they could be alone.

Instead, he'd minded his manners and taken the courtship slowly. By the time he mentioned his father, he figured it wouldn't be a problem. He'd almost lost Claire that day. She didn't consider herself an equal to the Blakes of Austin, which was ridiculous. Even worse, his father was marrying Megan Maitland this month. The grand dame of

Austin society and owner of the hospital that employed Claire was too much for Claire Goodman.

That had only been a week ago. He was still cautiously trying to get closer. In fact, he wanted in her bed. Since he intended to marry her anyway, he thought he was being reasonable.

He heard the outer door open and his head whipped up.

"Hello, Miss Goodman. Go right on in. Mr. Blake is waiting," his secretary, Carol, said.

Before Claire came into sight, Tom was out of his chair, around his desk, and racing to meet her. As she came through the door, he wrapped his arms around her and his lips met hers.

The kiss was like ambrosia to his soul. He'd starved for her. He hadn't even been able to call her. She'd insisted she'd be too busy.

With her enthusiastic participation, he considered going straight to the sofa, after closing the office door, but he held back, still not sure. "Man, I missed you," he whispered as he held her even closer.

"I—um, it's warm in here, isn't it?"

He leaned back, frowning. True, it was December, but Austin in December didn't mean freezing temperatures except on rare occasions. So the heat was on its lowest level. Her response was strange.

"Are you okay? Not coming down with anything?"

"No, I'm fine. I stopped by to tell you I can't have dinner with you tonight."

Before she'd left town, he'd made her promise to meet him for dinner tonight. He'd been looking forward to it all day. "Why not?"

She took several steps back. "Um, I've decided we—we shouldn't see each other anymore."

Only strong self-discipline and practice in court kept his legs from buckling. Maintaining a calm voice, he said, "Really? Why is that?"

She sent him an affronted look. "Well, obviously it doesn't matter to you anyway. But I don't think we want the same things."

Okay, so she wouldn't meet his gaze, which told him something wasn't kosher. "I suppose that's up for discussion, but shouldn't you ask me what I want before you condemn my choices?''

She moved closer to the door. ''It's pointless to discuss. I have to go.''

He'd followed her, slowly so he wouldn't scare her, but he reached out and caught her hand. ''You have another appointment?''

''Yes! I have another appointment.''

''Who with?''

''That's none of your business!'' Her cheeks were flushed.

''Well, I think it is since you're canceling our date.'' He knew he'd made a mistake as soon as he said the word *date*. She was signaling withdrawal with every word she used.

He pulled her closer. ''Who, Claire?''

Her agitation grew. ''It doesn't matter! I can't—it would be too awkward.''

''Because we're breaking up? Oh, no. I have a friendship policy with all my old girlfriends. Keeps me looking like a nice guy. Besides, I'm starving and I hate to eat alone. Come on, we'll grab a bite to eat and have a genteel discussion. It will be quite civil.''

Since she'd met one or two women he'd previously dated, maybe she'd believe that lie. He just knew that if he let her walk away tonight, he'd never convince her to go out with him again.

CLAIRE HAD KNOWN she wouldn't do this well. She'd wanted to be in and out in five minutes. Most of those five minutes had been spent in his arms, being thoroughly kissed. And she'd loved it. The man was an incredible kisser.

When she'd finally remembered she was rejecting him, he'd already stopped kissing her. Then, as if she hadn't dropped a bombshell, he'd accepted her decision with no protests. Just a request to go eat because he was starving.

And she'd thought he was sensitive!

He stepped back to his chair and grabbed the suit jacket on its back. "We'll just run to Mario's, nothing romantic, and grab some pasta."

Oh, sure! Nothing romantic! He knew she loved going to Mario's. He'd taken her there on their first date. The owner practically rolled out the red carpet for him and gave them a table that had since become their special one. The lights were always low, their table was a booth and Tom always sat next to her, whispering sweet things in her ears.

"I don't want to go to Mario's!" she lied.

"Mario would be upset to hear that. But the problem is, I don't know where we could get a table quickly in any other restaurant."

Claire scratched her forehead. Things weren't turning out the way she intended.

"And I am starving," he added, looking as pitiful as a handsome man could, his eyes wide and innocent.

"Oh, okay! But no—no acting like we're lovers for Mario's benefit," she warned him.

"That'll be easy, since we're not lovers. And if we were, it wouldn't be Mario who'd be smiling."

She ignored him and hurried out of his office.

Tom kept his eye on Claire as he drove them to Mario's. She'd wanted to drive herself, but he'd reminded her of the limited parking. She might be hurting Mario's business. Dirty pool, he knew, but he was desperate.

What was going on? Was it his family? They'd always been an asset before. His father was one of the leading corporate attorneys in Austin, representing Maitland Maternity as well as other large companies.

His two sisters had their idiosyncrasies, but they'd welcomed Claire with easy friendliness. "Did you see Diane as you came in today?"

"Yes. I know you can't tell me about the problem, but is everything all right for Whitney? She has so much to bear already."

He found Claire's sympathy admirable. He'd known women who sneered at teenagers who got pregnant. Not Claire. "I think everything will be okay."

"Good."

"Will you take care of her babies?"

"If they're underweight. I only deal with the special babies. If they're healthy and both over five pounds, they'll go in the regular nursery."

"Did you go straight to the hospital after you got off the plane?"

"Yes, of course. And we got three new babies while I was gone. Two of them are already on the verge of being transferred out, but the other one— Well, it will be a few days."

He noticed the tension had lessened while

they discussed her beloved job. Good. He'd have a better chance of finding out what was going on, if she was relaxed.

When Mario showed them to their special table, beaming, Tom thanked him and then slid around the half circle to Claire's side.

She glared at him and shifted away from him. "You promised."

"How can we talk if we're separated? You know how noisy it gets in here."

She shifted farther away.

The waiter came to the table and asked, "The usual?"

Tom nodded and the man left before Claire could speak.

"Wait!" she called, but the waiter was too far away to hear her.

"You want something different?"

"Yes, but it's too late."

"No, it's not. I'll go get him if you want to order something else." She'd been ordering the same thing from the first day, but a lady had the right to change.

"Never mind," she said, scooting along the seat again. "It doesn't matter."

They sat there in silence, and all the tension he'd erased in the car was back full force.

"Have you met someone else?" he abruptly asked, unable to hold back.

"No! I mean, well, um, I met a lot of people at the conference." She wasn't looking at him again.

"You know that's not what I mean."

"I can change my mind without having met someone new, can't I?" she said, sticking out her stubborn chin.

"Of course. I just want to know why. You know how I feel about you, and I thought you felt the same about me."

Her hands were shaking, and he decided to ease the tension again. Snapping his fingers, he said, "Oh, damn! I'd forgotten!"

He'd snagged her attention. "What?"

"I was counting on you to help me out. Now what will I do?" He was frantically thinking up a project for her.

"I'm sure you'll manage on your own."

"I would if it wasn't a female thing. You know I'm not good at those things." He stretched his arm out on the back of the seat and leaned toward her.

"What female thing? I've never seen you—"

"Sure you have. When I gave a present to my sister and it was still in the sack. You said I should've had it wrapped. I hadn't even thought about it."

"They have gift wrapping in the stores," she pointed out. "Problem solved."

"I know that, but the problem was I didn't think of it. Anyway, I want to do something special for Dad and Megan. I was going to ask you to help me. I want to host a party for them Friday evening."

"This is ridiculous. You can get someone to help."

"I decided too late. It's the holiday season and no one can handle it. I've got our housekeeper's help, but I need some assistance making decisions. I don't have much time."

"No, you don't, but it's not my problem."

"In a way, it's your fault, though. I decided to do this just after you left town. I waited until you got home to work on it because I needed your advice."

"You are not going to blame me for—"

He interrupted her. "Of course not. But

all I'm asking for is a little advice. It will be over Friday night. Can't you put off disappearing out of my life until then? Is that asking so much?''

"Tom, I don't live on your social scale. Your sisters would be better at—''

"Diane is responsible for Whitney, and you know that's time-consuming, plus she's a bridesmaid. Suzanne is planning her wedding and is a bridesmaid and will be a new mother three times over. What more do you want from them?''

He held his breath, waiting to see if he'd convinced her to hang around a little longer.

CHAPTER TWO

THE PROBLEM, Claire realized, was she didn't want to go away. She didn't want to lose Tom. And his reasons did sound sort of legitimate. She knew the Christmas season was crazy for the social set in Austin. When you add to that the biggest wedding of the year, well, things could get difficult.

"I'll help you as a friend," she said hurriedly, before he changed his mind.

"Bless you," he said with a smile. Then he leaned over and kissed her. He kept it brief, leaving her hungry, so she couldn't complain.

"I don't suppose you could take off a couple of days, say, Thursday and Friday, for last minute details?"

"I—I could." She had some vacation days available.

"Perfect! Now, tell me why you're breaking up with me."

The sudden change of subject left her head spinning.

"Uh, it's like I said. We don't want the same things."

"I don't agree, because what I want, more than anything, is you."

"Me?" she quaked, surprised by his response.

"You," he assured her and immediately kissed her as he had when she'd entered the office.

She was breathing heavily when he pulled back. Damn! She couldn't turn him away. Not when she was as hungry for him as he was for her. "Don't touch me! You promised."

"Sorry, I forgot."

The waiter arrived with their order.

For the next several minutes, they both concentrated on their meal as if they really were hungry. Then he tried again.

"Is it bad breath? B.O.? Did you see me with another woman?"

Her gaze leveled on him. "Have you been with another woman?"

He held up a hand. "Not since I laid eyes

on you, sweetheart. I think you've ruined me for all other women.''

"Don't be ridiculous! I'm just—just normal.''

Tom threw back his head and laughed out loud. When he stopped laughing, he took her chin between his fingers and said, "Not to me, you're not. I think our being together is fate, Claire. You're the best thing that ever happened to me.''

She was shaking badly all over. "No, no, no. That can't be. Please, Tom, just—just let me go.''

Now he was getting worried. He slid his arm around her shoulders and pulled her against him and with his other hand, he clasped hers. "Sweetheart, what's wrong? Tell me what's wrong and I'll fix it.''

She buried her face in his jacket and shook her head no. "You c-can't.''

"Well, you could at least explain why, so I'll be prepared next time.''

"Your sister told me.''

Friday night, he'd taken Claire to his sister's house for drinks, showing Claire they were all regular folks. He figured Suzanne, with her soon-to-be new mother duties, would be just a little bit harried.

He hadn't counted on any family secrets revealed. And he was afraid he knew which one had been put on parade. "Did she congratulate you for being so broadminded as to pair yourself off with a sterile man?"

"S-something like that."

His sister had no business preempting his right to inform her of his problem. But he knew Suzanne hadn't meant to break his confidence. She wouldn't do that.

"I would've told you before we went much further, honey, I promise. But there are so many possibilities today, I thought if we cared for each other, something could be worked out."

When he was eighteen, shortly after his mother passed away, Tom got the mumps. It wasn't until later on that he discovered the effects of the disease—sterility. Tom battled depression for several years, but was fortunate enough to have the love and support of his father and his mother's sister, Katie. They had both taught him to count his blessings and look at alternatives since he could now not bear children of his own. At his father's suggestion, Tom took a great interest in helping children—he organized sports like basketball and baseball within the city and even became a Big brother when he was in college. Through these activities and relationships, Tom came to accept that not being able to have children of his own did not at all mean he couldn't ever enjoy their company. Tom knew it was a subject to be broached carefully and could shock the woman who first heard it.

"Wouldn't one of those other alternatives do?"

"You see," she began, wiping her face with the back of her hand, "I've always had this dream of having the perfect husband, the perfect child. I know it's silly but—" She broke off and swallowed. "When she told me that Friday night, I panicked. It was all I could think of all weekend. I decided it would be easier to give you up. Only—it's hard." She looked away. "Besides, we already had the social thing."

She hoped that last would distract him, knowing her words didn't make sense. And she couldn't explain it either, this illogical primal instinct that urged her to have the perfect home with a child from her own body. It was crazy, and she hated that she felt this way. But logic or not, she needed to have a baby of her own.

"What social thing?" he asked quickly.

"You know I'm not a jet-setter," she explained impatiently.

"Neither am I." He watched her carefully before he said, "Look, you've promised me a week. Let's not make any decisions until next weekend. Maybe you'll be able to rethink your decision."

"I don't think—"

"I think it would be wise of you. And there are some advantages. You know I can't get you pregnant, so you don't have to worry about me getting anyone else pregnant."

She raised her head to give him an outraged look. But at least she wasn't still crying. He'd purposely tried to shock her. He added hurriedly, "I wouldn't, I promise. In fact, let me take you home tonight and show you how faithful I can be."

Her smile was sweet, but she said no. Then, sitting up, she asked to go. The evening had exhausted her.

He could understand why. He'd thought

he could handle his disability but he couldn't if it meant losing Claire.

TOM HAD SPENT most of the night trying to determine the problem. Other than the obvious one—him. The only guess he'd had was that Claire didn't think she could love someone else's baby.

So here he was this morning, standing in the shadows, watching Claire at work—and he knew he'd been wrong. Every little scrap of humanity in that glassed-in room fighting for life had a staunch supporter in Claire. The love poured out of her as she touched them through the rubber gloves attached to the incubators. She stroked them, sang to them, talked to them, her whole being concentrating on giving them the strength to make it.

Now, she'd taken one of the largest babies, obviously nearly ready to be transferred to the regular nursery, into her arms and was feeding him his bottle. Tom couldn't hear through the glass walls, but the rocker moved back and forth and so did her lips, either singing or talking to the baby.

Tom couldn't even picture Claire turning

her back on a baby because it wasn't hers. There was just too much love in her. So, if that wasn't the problem, what was? There had to be something in her past that was the key to what was happening.

Normally, he'd wait and hope she'd confess whatever it was that had convinced her to make the decision to stop seeing him. But he only had five days. He'd have to force the issue, but he dreaded doing it.

Claire wouldn't like it, but he was desperate. He might not be able to physically father children, but he had every intention of raising a family, and he wanted Claire by his side.

He took one last look at Claire in her own little world, doing her best for the babies. Yeah, he wanted Claire, for all time. With or without babies. And he wanted her to want him, too.

CLAIRE LOVED HER WORK. And she was pleased when a baby made such progress that it could go home with its mama. But she also hated saying goodbye. Today Snoopy was going home. His real name was Barry Lionel Richmond—such a big name for a little one, so the nurses called him Snoopy. He'd been born two months early weighing just over three pounds. Now he was fully developed and topped the scales at five pounds and one ounce.

"You're going to be the best thing in your mommy's stocking for Christmas, Snoopy. I want you to keep growing, you hear? You're going to get lots bigger if you'll just keep taking your milk."

She briskly wrapped him in his blankets, making sure his knitted cap was in place, trying to keep the tears at bay. The other nurses told her she was too emotional. Maybe so, but each of the babies seemed to become a part of her.

"Here you are, Mrs. Richmond," she said as she placed Snoopy in his mother's arms. "Your healthy baby."

"Thank you so much for your care of him."

Her supervisor whispered, as the parents walked away, "Take your lunch break now. Cassie just came on."

With a sigh, she nodded and left the preemie area to go down to the cafeteria. She wasn't feeling particularly hungry, but she knew better than to skip meals.

After choosing from the cafeteria offerings, she settled down at a table by the windows and pulled her cell phone out of her purse. It wouldn't take but a minute to check her messages at the apartment.

Within a minute, she'd snatched up her purse and walked away from a tray full of food, heading in a rage to Tom's law office.

She couldn't believe he would leave a message like that on her machine, telling her she had no choice about seeing him that night. He thought he could make decisions for her? Tell her what she was going to do? Maybe she was overreacting, but even if she helped him with the party, that didn't mean he could control her life!

Fortunately, when she arrived at his nearby offices, he was eating lunch at his desk. She wasn't prepared to wait. "How dare you?" she demanded as she burst through his door, his secretary hovering behind her.

He acknowledged his secretary first. "It's okay, Carol. Close the door for me. Thanks."

Once they were alone, he turned to stare at her, and she felt like an idiot with that dramatic entrance.

"How dare I what?"

"Think you can arrange my schedule. You could've *asked* if I was free. Just because I'm not your social equal doesn't mean you can take me for granted!"

He frowned at her. "You know I don't buy into that social crap. But I only have five days to convince you we're perfect together. I want us to talk. I want to find out why you're intent on breaking my heart."

He crossed the room to her side, wrapped his arms around her and whispered, "I'm sorry, sweetheart, if I came across as dictatorial."

His embrace felt so good, the warmth and concern in his voice so healing, Claire had difficulty fighting the tears. She loved him so much. But he was right—she had a secret, and it was time she told him so he'd understand. With determination, she finally disclosed the truth. "I had a baby—when I was fifteen. He's almost that age now."

"At fifteen? That's pretty young." He

pulled her a little closer. "What happened to the baby?"

"He—he was adopted. That's all I know."

"I'm sorry, sweetheart. But I'm not sure I understand how this information affects us."

She backed out of his embrace and stared at him. "Do you think your family and friends would want you to marry me if they knew about my secret?"

He stared back at her, honestly surprised. "Why would it be any of their business?"

"Because your family is part of the elite of Austin," she reminded him, thinking it was obvious.

"Claire, I understand how losing your child would affect you. But other than knowing it caused you pain, it doesn't affect me. And I find it hard to believe that the woman I love would reject me because I can't have a baby with her. Especially not a woman who pours out all her love every day, to the babies in the hospital."

Claire sniffed and turned her back to him to wipe away the tears that had insisted on running down her cheeks. "I—I promised myself when I had to give up my little boy that one day I'd have a baby, my husband and I, and provide the perfect home…to make up for giving him away. That dream became so important to me. When I met you I thought—'' She broke off, unable to keep going.

He drew her back into his arms, as if he knew she needed to borrow his strength. She nestled against him, knowing it was unfair to do so, when she didn't plan a future with him, but somehow she couldn't stop herself.

He moved them to the sofa. She relaxed in his arms, recuperating from the adrenaline that had kept her going. ''What are you doing here, by the way? Aren't you supposed to be at work?''

''Yes, I was having lunch. But I was so upset after getting your message, that I couldn't think about food and left the tray behind on the table.'' She regretted that now as her stomach gurgled in protest.

He got up and crossed to his desk, bringing back the sandwich and chips he'd been eating. ''Fortunately, I didn't get too far with this sandwich before you got here.''

It was a roast beef sandwich from a deli around the corner.

"I can't eat your lunch!" she protested.

"Don't be silly. I'll order another one later. You can't order in from the nursery."

Unable to resist, she took a bite. And another.

Tom introduced the subject of the Friday night party, taking her mind off what had brought her there. Soon he had her laughing at his fears and protesting his ridiculous plans. As was his intention.

The man could lift the spirits of a bear with a thorn in its paw. She sighed as she leaned against him. "You're too good to me, Tom. But now you understand why I said I wasn't good enough to—to be a part of the group you socialize with."

"No, why?"

"Oh, come on, Tom. An unwed mother at fifteen? I don't think so."

"Megan Maitland was an unwed mother, too. Her father told her her baby died and then sold it to her future sister-in-law."

Claire stared at him in horror. "No! No one could be so cruel!"

"It's the truth. Now me, I'm perfect, of

course, but the rest of that social crowd have all kinds of secrets!'' he assured her with a grin. She poked him in his ribs.

''Ow! I'm a sensitive guy. Be careful.''

She laughed as she returned her head to his shoulder. ''You are a wonderful person, Tom Blake. And I adore you,'' she added in a soft whisper.

His arms tightened around her. ''Good. That's exactly what I want. A woman who will forgive me anything. Fortunately, I feel the same way about you.''

''I shouldn't have said that! I was thinking out loud. Really, Tom, you should find someone who'll fit in better.''

''I can't think of anyone who would fit me better.'' He pulled her tighter against him, his lips covering hers and his hands stroking her body beneath the crisp nurse's uniform.

''Damn! Couldn't you wear a soft nightie to visit me? It would make life so much simpler,'' he teased when he finally released her.

Almost breathless with passion, she sat up and put herself in order. ''I think you need to move on, find someone more—more accommodating, Tom.''

He kissed her again, a brief hard kiss to punctuate his words. ''I'm not moving on, Claire. We belong to each other.''

''But—''

''Nope, no arguments. By the way, I have a question for you.''

''What?'

''Would you like to adopt Whitney's babies?''

CHAPTER THREE

"WE CAN'T DO THAT!" she exclaimed, her face pale.

Tom watched her closely. "Why not?"

"We're—we're not even married. We'd have to be married before anyone would consider letting us adopt any baby."

"That's true," he said consideringly, as if he'd never thought of that problem. Then he grinned at her. "But I know a judge. We could get married this afternoon."

"But I just said I was going to break up with you! Did you forget?"

"How can you break up with me, sweetheart, when you just said you adore me." His smile changed from teasing to loving and he kissed her gently.

"Tom, I don't know what to do," she suddenly wailed, jumping up from the sofa.

"You don't have to do anything, Claire. I wasn't trying to put pressure on you. And if we don't take Whitney's babies, there will be other babies needing homes. There always are. But I admire Whitney. She's got guts."

"That's just it. I'm not sure she should give them up!"

"Fair enough."

"That doesn't mean I wouldn't want to—I'd love to—but we'd have to marry at once and I'm not sure that's what we should do!" She began pacing the floor.

"I've been sure for weeks," he said calmly, still watching her.

That stopped her in her tracks. "How can you say that? We've only known each other about eight weeks."

"I was sure after two." He smiled.

"This is not a contest, Tom! We're talking about our lives." She put her hands on her hips, as if she were scolding him.

He stood and crossed to her, looping his hands around her waist. "I know. I'm a quick study."

She gave him a look of disgust. "I think you're crazy."

"Just think about it for a while. So, about tonight…I'll pick you up from the hospital this afternoon. We can run by your place so you can change. Then we'll go to my dad's, so you can get some ideas about the decor.''

"The decor? I thought I just had to come up with a menu and—I'm not good with decor,'' she assured him, trying to back away.

He chuckled. "Don't worry about it. We'll hang mistletoe. Come on, I'll run you back to the hospital so you won't be late.''

A quick look at her watch chased all the other thoughts from her head. She was never late.

BEFORE HE PICKED Claire up that afternoon, Tom did some thinking. He had a question or two to ask her, but he thought he'd figured out the problem. She thought it was because she had a baby when she was only a child herself. That wasn't what he thought.

As much as Claire had told herself having another baby would take away her pain of losing her first child, Tom didn't believe it. He wanted Claire, but most of all, he wanted Claire to be happy. Even if she decided to walk away, he thought she'd need to resolve the issue of her first child. Not try to replace him with another baby.

But that would have to be her decision, not his. And who knew how long it would take, even if she decided this evening to find her baby.

In the meantime, he warned his father that he and Claire would be there that evening. By the time he went to get Claire, the evening had turned into a tree-decorating party. His father had ordered a large Scotch pine to be delivered. Mrs. Dee, the housekeeper, would provide a buffet so they could mix decorating with eating, and both his sisters would be on hand. They never missed decorating the tree.

Sometimes it was hard to get into the Christmas spirit in Austin what with sunshine and no snow in sight. But Tom felt it coming on. He was pretty sure this Christmas was going to be a spectacular one.

Claire had just come out of the hospital when he stopped the car. "Want a ride, lady?" he asked in his best snake oil salesman voice.

She fluttered her eyelashes and cooed. "Why, how gentlemanly of you, but my mama said never to accept rides from strangers."

"Ah. I'd introduce myself but the cops are after me and I'm short of time. Jump in!"

"Okay!" she agreed and did so. They both broke into laughter as he pulled away from the curb. Her sense of the ridiculous was one of the things he enjoyed most about her.

He picked up her hand and carried it to his lips. "You're going to have to do a better job teaching our daughters about such things."

"How true. We wouldn't want them— Tom, we haven't agreed—never mind."

He grinned. He was getting to her. Tonight should help his cause. He and his dad talked about a lot of things that afternoon, changes he needed to make if he was about to become a husband and father. He couldn't wait.

At Claire's modest apartment, he followed her in and paced her small living room as she dashed back to her bedroom. "I'm assuming casual, right?" she called.

"Yeah, casual. Mrs. Dee will fix eats and we'll decorate the tree and the house and eat while we're doing it."

"What a luxury! How long has Mrs. Dee been with your family?" The disembodied voice floated into the room. Tom hesitated, because he hadn't intended to tell her now, but the opportunity seemed right.

"About twenty years. She's wonderful. I thought maybe she'd work for us once we're married."

No response came floating back. Instead, Claire, her short blond hair all ruffled from pulling a knit shirt over it, walked to the door to stare at him. "What did you say?"

"I said I thought maybe Mrs. Dee, whose real name by the way is Detrosky, might work for us when we're married."

"Why, *if* we got married, would I need a housekeeper? That's ridiculous."

"Is it? Do you think we could move into your apartment or mine?"

"Why couldn't we move into my apartment?"

"With twins? If Whitney should agree to our adopting her twins, where would we put them?" He smiled and watched her realize what he was talking about.

"Well, I— It might not happen. We could—" She put her hands on her slender hips and stared at him, frustration filling her. "Things don't happen overnight, Tom."

"They could for us. It would just take two stubborn ladies saying yes, you and Whitney."

"Good heavens," she said, sinking into a nearby chair. "It could happen, couldn't it? Not that I think Whitney is stubborn, but it's a big decision. She wants to do the right thing."

"As do I. So I talked to Dad about buying his house," he added, hoping she wouldn't notice that piece of news, but he wanted to say it before she saw the house. "That's why you'd need Mrs. Dee."

She picked up on it at once. "Buy your father's house?"

"Yeah, you'll see it tonight. It's old, but Dad's maintained it well."

"Why isn't Mrs. Maitland moving into the house?"

Tom grinned. "Because hers is bigger and she's happy there."

She frowned and stood. "I'll finish getting ready." Then she disappeared back into her room.

Tom drew a deep breath. That had gone

better than he'd feared. Of course, she hadn't seen his dad's house. He hadn't lived at home in ten years, but he knew it was a great house for kids. He'd grown up there. Lots of yard to play in, plenty of space for every child, and a huge kitchen. He hoped Claire agreed with him.

She reappeared, a serious expression in her eyes.

Finally, she asked, "When are we supposed to be there?"

"Whenever. My sisters will be over around seven, but we've got to get the lights straightened out and organize the decorations. I'll have to do that because sometimes they don't get separated before they're put up."

"Separated from what?"

He grinned. "You were an only child, weren't you? Every year we each added to our collection of ornaments. And death to anyone but us who hung our ornaments. Now, they're supposed to be packed in separate boxes, but sometimes one goes astray."

"Really?" She seemed in shock at such behavior.

"Yeah. Every one of the ornaments holds a lot of memories. The year after Mom died, we cried the entire time we decorated the tree, but our memories brought her alive for a few hours." He sighed. "It was wonderful."

He discovered Claire in his arms, burying her face in his chest, and he hugged her close. Clearing his throat, he said, "Yeah, and that's the kind of Christmas I want us to have every year, sweetheart. One that celebrates the gifts we've been given."

"That sounds wonderful," she whispered, lifting her lips for a kiss that he gladly bestowed on her. In fact, he became so enthusiastic about it, he almost forgot they had to go.

"Damn, never the time and place," he muttered, leaning his forehead against hers.

"We'd better go," Claire whispered, but she didn't pull away.

"We could forget the Christmas tree and—"

"That would be a terribly rude thing to do to your family. They'd never like me."

"They already adore you, even Dad

who's never met you. He didn't think anyone would take me on.''

She pushed away from him. ''Oh, right.
Poor Thomas Blake. No one wanted him.
He's so ugly, so broke, so degenerate.
Right!''

He grinned. ''Yes, you've saved me,'' he
exclaimed, using his high school drama
techniques.

With a sigh, she ordered, ''Let's just go.
And be glad you don't have to rely on your
acting ability to make a living.''

Conversation disappeared again until he
pulled into the drive that circled in front of
his father's house.

''This is your father's house? The one that
you offered to buy?'' she asked, her eyes
wide.

''Yeah,'' he said carelessly, hoping to off-
set the awe in her voice.

Instead of getting out, she turned and
stared at him. ''Just how rich are you,
Thomas Blake?''

CLAIRE DIDN'T EXPECT an answer, didn't
even want to know the details of his finan-
cial situation. But the house was enor-

mous…and gorgeous. She fell in love with it at once, but it would be a pipe dream to think that she might ever be mistress of such a place.

Or that she'd know what to do with it.

"I need to return home, Tom. I can't stay," she muttered, staring straight ahead.

"Oh, no, you don't. No backing out on me now."

"No, I'm serious. This whole—whole situation is beyond my means, my capabilities." She stubbornly remained in place.

He got out of the car and came around to open the door. Then he said, "You can either walk in or I'll carry you, little lady. If I carry you, they'll think you've accepted my proposal. What will it be?"

She couldn't face any congratulations. With a look of horror on her face, she jumped out of the car. Then she realized another problem. "Oh, my heavens! You let me dress in jeans to come here."

"What's wrong with that?" he asked, a puzzled look on his face.

"I should at least be dressed in wool trousers, a cashmere twin set with a string of pearls." Didn't the man know anything?

"I think you've watched too many reruns of *Dallas,* Claire. Real people don't live like that," he assured her while pulling her after him to the front door. After ringing the doorbell, he opened the door himself and entered into a long, cool foyer. The Mexican tile covered with various oriental rugs, paintings on the walls and an antique entry table was a beautiful combination.

"Oh, my heavens!" Claire whispered.

"Hey, it's just the entryway, Claire. No big deal." He continued to move them along, toward the back of the house.

She didn't take another breath until they entered a huge kitchen, bright, cheerful, and, except for its size, normal. The lady standing at the sink turned and smiled at Tom. "Hi, there. I didn't hear you come in. Ready for coffee and a snack?"

"Yeah, that'd be good. And Mrs. Dee, here's Claire."

The woman took her hand in both of hers. "Welcome, Claire. I hope you don't mind if I call you Claire?"

"Of course not," Claire assured her.

"Good, sit at the breakfast bar and we can

chat while you eat. I've still got some work to do for the buffet.''

As Claire sat on a tall kitchen stool sipping coffee, she actually began to feel at home with Mrs. Dee. Tom was putting away a lot of food while they talked, and she watched him out of the corner of her eye. ''Does he always eat like this?'' she finally asked.

Tom looked up. ''Hey!'' he protested. ''Someone ate my lunch today.''

Claire had completely forgotten that part of her day since so much had already happened. ''Oh! I'd forgotten that. I'm so sorry, Tom. Didn't you order another lunch? You said you would.''

Mrs. Dee nodded to Tom. ''Shame on you, Thomas.''

Claire looked at each of them puzzled. ''What do you mean?''

''You're sweet. But you've got to not let this guy take advantage of you. He may have missed lunch but it was because he knew he'd fill up over here. He didn't suffer any.''

''But Mrs. Dee, he did give up his lunch for me. Even after I interrupted him in the middle of the day.'' Thinking about her behavior now, Claire was embarrassed.

"But, dear, it's a man's job to take care of his loved ones.'' The housekeeper continued preparing a vegetable tray, as if Tom had only done what he was supposed to do.

But Claire knew better. Tom's behavior since she'd come back from the weekend had been more than patient. Incredibly so.

Suddenly a dynamic man entered the kitchen and stuck out his hand toward Claire. "Well, well, this must be the incredible Claire, my future daughter-in-law. Welcome to the family!''

CHAPTER FOUR

TOM CRINGED and clenched his hands together to keep from choking his father. "Uh, Dad, I told you—"

"I know," Hugh protested with easy charm, charm that wasn't going anywhere with Claire. "You told me nothing was settled, but how could she resist you, son?"

Claire slid off the stool and said, "Sorry, if I— I really should go. It's nice to have met you."

She turned to Tom, as if she expected him to show her the front door.

"You're not going anywhere," he said roughly. "You promised."

"But Tom, obviously your father has expectations that—" She broke off when he put his hands around her waist and lifted her back on the stool.

"My father, in his misguided way, was trying to sway your decision." Tom stopped and glared at his father again. "Besides, he's one of those parents that can't imagine anyone being able to resist his offspring."

Hugh shrugged. "Well, it's true, they can't. You've always had success with—"

"Dad! Your conversation is not helping!"

But some of the tension eased from Claire. "Hmm, I think his conversation is just getting interesting." A smile flirted with her lips.

Tom smacked those same lips with his. "Nope, that conversation isn't going to happen."

"Oh, so you do have things to hide?" Claire teased, before remembering she'd decided to walk away from the man. She quickly ducked her head.

Tom grinned. "Absolutely nothing…as long as you don't talk to my family."

Both Hugh and Mrs. Dee laughed but Claire only smiled. Then she turned to Tom's father. "I'm helping Tom out with your party, but I'm not joining the family. I'd love to stay to decorate, but not if it makes you uncomfortable."

After a quick look at Tom, Hugh smiled. "Not at all. We're delighted to have you.

And I hope my mistake didn't embarrass you.''

Claire politely assured him she was fine.

Tom looked at his father. "Is Megan coming?"

"No, she already had a commitment. You know how busy everyone is during the Christmas season."

Tom nodded with a grimace and dragged Claire off to the living room where the tree had been delivered earlier.

He hadn't wanted to start in that room because it had a formality that might've put her off. There were several conversational groupings, each around a large oriental rug. The walls had several remarkable pieces of art and the crystal lamps were museum quality.

Claire stopped beside one of them, barely touching the lamp, and said, "Is this an actual Tiffany lamp?"

"Mmm-hmm. What do you think of the tree?"

She turned to look at the Scotch pine that stood in the corner. "Why, it's huge! How ever will you decorate it?"

He grinned. "Very carefully!" After eyeing it a minute longer, he said, "I'm going to get a couple of ladders. You find Mrs. Dee and ask her to help you bring down the ornament boxes. And see if she picked up some candy canes today."

And he hurried away.

THE HOUSE ITSELF was incredible. Claire had been able to forget that for a few minutes chatting with the housekeeper in the kitchen. But now, staring at the antiques and beautiful furniture in the living room, she again felt completely out of place.

Her gaze kept returning to the big green tree standing in the corner. Since she'd had her baby Christmas had never been the same. She'd told herself it was because she was an adult now. She shouldn't expect magic. It had been a holiday she'd celebrated as little as possible.

These people with their money and their beautiful home, truly went to a great deal of trouble to celebrate Christmas. She supposed it was easier for them because they could just hire someone to do it all, but she didn't think that's what they did.

She heard the sound of a door closing

somewhere. It reminded her that Tom expected her to retrieve the boxes of ornaments. Not wanting to be thought lazy, she hurried back to the kitchen to help Mrs. Dee.

In the kitchen, she discovered Diane and Whitney with Mrs. Dee. "I didn't hear you come in," she exclaimed, puzzled.

"Oh, we came in through the garage," Diane assured her. "It's actually started raining."

"Oh, I had no idea it was going to rain."

"I was hoping for snow," Whitney added.

Even Mr. Blake laughed at that wistful hope. "I think you'll need to move farther north to have a white Christmas."

"Maybe I will," Whitney said.

"You can choose a college up north," Diane suggested. "I know several good ones."

"But it will be difficult with twins," Tom added softly, from the doorway where he stood with two ladders leaning against the wall.

Diane glared at her brother. "She hasn't decided yet!"

"I know. But I want her to be realistic." He really hadn't meant to come across callously. Tom was concerned for what was best for all.

Claire suddenly remembered Tom's suggestion that they become the parents of Whitney's twins. Her gaze glued itself to Whitney's stomach and a longing she hadn't expected surged in her. "Uh, do you know if you're having boys or girls?"

"Boys," Whitney said with a twist of her lips. "I wanted girls."

Claire actually clutched her hands together to keep from reaching out to touch the precious burden Whitney carried. "The sex of the babies doesn't matter much."

"Either one's a lot of work," Mrs. Dee added softly, not looking at Whitney. She started to say something else, but Tom frowned at her.

Claire looked first at Mrs. Dee and then Tom, who was still standing by the door. He was trying to be sensitive about Whitney's situation.

Tom interrupted her thoughts. "Did you get the ornaments?"

"Oh! No, I came in here and discovered Diane and Whitney and—and I forgot," she explained.

"Boy, some assistant you're going to be," he claimed with a grin. Then he shouldered the two ladders and headed to the living room.

Mrs. Dee said, "The boxes are behind the purple-striped settee in the corner. Just go pull them out and show him how efficient you are," she directed with a smile.

Claire thanked her and, followed by Diane and Whitney, she charged after Tom. As he set up the two stepladders, she and Diane got out the boxes. Then she said breathlessly, "Here they are!"

"Good. Thanks," he murmured, as if his mind were only focused on the tree.

Diane removed the cover from one of the boxes. "Oh! This is my box. Come see, Whitney!"

Claire found a grocery sack filled with large candy canes, ready to be put on the tree. She loved peppermint and knew the candy canes would be her favorite part of the decorations.

"Stop inhaling the candy canes and come help me straighten out the lights," Tom ordered, smiling at her. "They have to go on first. Then the angel. After that, it's a free-for-all.''

"Isn't Suzanne coming?" Diane called from where she was sorting through ornaments.

"Yeah. I think she's bringing her fiancé and his daughters. Said they'd enjoy decorating the tree."

Diane looked smug. "I got them together."

Tom gave her a brotherly look. "Then I hope it doesn't turn out to be a disaster. Matchmaking can be tricky."

"I know, but they seem perfect together," Diane said, her tones serious.

Claire thought about her childhood. How much she'd wanted a sibling. How much she'd wanted a holiday table with family and friends gathered around. Instead, it was always just the three of them. Her father eager to get to the television set, her mother wanting to get the mess cleaned up. And her.

"Okay, Claire. I'm going to climb the ladder, and you hold up the first part of the lights so I can put them in the branches," Tom directed. She did as he said and in a few minutes the huge tree was wrapped in lights.

Tom climbed down. "Now, for the test!" he announced, as if he were presenting a magic show. Claire held her breath, wanting his work to be perfect.

She shouldn't have worried. The entire tree was covered with small, white twinkling lights, like distant stars in the universe. She clapped her hands together. "Oh, Tom, you did a perfect job! How beautiful!"

Tom hugged her. "Just what I want, a lady who thinks I'm perfect."

His sister's derisive laughter didn't even phase Claire, who received his kiss without protest this time. The front doorbell, a huge sound that rang through the house, broke them apart.

"What's that?" she asked.

"It's our gong. Quaint, isn't it?" Diane asked with a grin. "When I had to ring the doorbell to get in because I was late, I dreaded hearing that noise."

"I can imagine." Claire shuddered.

Hugh Blake appeared to introduce his oldest daughter and her guests. Claire had met Suzanne before and while she'd heard about

Suzanne's fiancé, she'd never met him or his daughters. He was handsome, tall, and clearly adoring of Suzanne. His four-year-old daughters—Kimmie, Fran and Edie—were dressed in matching red dresses, and their hair in identical ponytails. Triplets.

Claire stared at them, delight on her face. She couldn't wait to get close to them.

"You're just in time," Tom called. "The tree's ready, and it's hard to hold this crowd back."

For the next half hour, chaos reigned, with side trips to the kitchen for snacks. Claire was glad to see that no one ate in the living room, but they all moved freely, uninhibited by their surroundings.

And the tree began to take shape. As each of the Blake children pulled out a favorite ornament, he or she told the newcomers about it and why it meant so much. It was an illuminating recital of family history that seemed so rich to Claire. She helped Tom hang some of his. He enlisted the triplets to help him, too.

The tree was being trimmed to perfection. Just when Claire thought it needed nothing else, Tom stepped in front of her, a wrapped gift in his hands.

"What's this?" she asked, puzzled.

"Open it, you'll see."

Much to her embarrassment, everyone in the room stopped to watch her. When she lifted the lid, embossed with a famous crystal company's name, she discovered a baby Jesus in a manger.

"Hang it on the tree, Claire," Tom urged, giving her a little push toward it.

Claire stared at the baby, tracing its cuddly shape with her finger, knowing Tom had bought the ornament because of her own baby, giving her permission to let her baby share in Christmas. Tears filled her eyes so she could scarcely see the tree. "Tom, I can't see—"

He stepped to her side and wrapped his arms around her. "Come on, Claire, I'll help." He guided her fingers to an empty branch and slipped the ornament on it. "There. Now you have part interest in our tree, too," he whispered, kissing her cheek. They backed away from the tree to admire it all.

Hugh passed out the candy canes to the

little girls and they began hanging them on the tree. But their height put them at a disadvantage. So Hugh, Tom and their dad each lifted the little girls high in the air, amid shrieks of excitement, so they could hang the candy canes higher.

Just as they finished, Mrs. Dee carried in a silver tray with silver punch cups filled with warm apple cider. Hugh strode to the tray and lifted a cup. "A toast to Christmas," he announced. "Everyone get a cup."

After a few minutes, they were ready. He lifted his cup. "To Christmas, a joyous time of the year to bring family close, to remember the good times, to create better ones for the future, to give thanks for the blessings given. Amen."

Soft Christmas music played in the background. Tom took Claire's cup from her hands, then wrapped his arms around her. Together they stared at the beautiful tree before them.

Claire, for the first time in fifteen years, felt all the things Christmas was supposed to make one feel. Her heart swelled with love and thanksgiving, and she felt like singing.

One hand stole up to caress Tom's cheek. He kissed her palm and pulled her tighter against him.

This moment would forever be a place of joy in her heart.

TOM HELD Claire close. He prayed she would see how perfect they were together. Christmas had never meant as much to him as it did tonight, with her in his arms.

But they had some rocky times ahead of them. He asked her if she was ready to leave. She nodded, but she wore a surprised look on her beautiful face. But he had to get her alone so they would talk again about her decision.

Once they were in the car, he began. "Claire, the men you've dated, did they break up with you?"

She looked at him in surprise. "What are you talking about?"

"Did you break up with them, or they with you?"

Silence fell, as if she were counting back. Finally, she said, "I usually broke up with them. Why? What does it matter?"

"I've been doing some thinking. I'm

wondering if you're punishing yourself for giving up your child. If your decision isn't about your dream, but about your feeling you don't deserve to be happy.''

She turned to stare at him, shock on her face. ''I don't—I couldn't avoid giving away my child. My father made me!''

''I know that. And I think you believe that, but I'm not sure you've forgiven yourself for not being able to do something about it.''

''What are you, a damn psychologist? You don't know what you're talking about!'' she exclaimed, but he noted tears filling her eyes.

''Don't I? Your dream is a nice one. But not logical. I think you could do even more good by giving a loving home to a child who doesn't have one. Trust me. I saw and got to know many kids who would love to have you for a mom. You're so loving. Wouldn't that make more sense? Making up for one child losing his home by taking in another one? You're too smart not to have thought of that.''

''I don't see it that way.'' But she didn't face him.

"I'm not trying to upset you, Claire. But I love you and I want us to have a future together. I don't think you'll let yourself be happy until you find your son and make sure he's happy."

"What if he isn't?" Her voice was shaking and he definitely knew tears were falling.

"Is that why you haven't tried to find him? Because you were afraid of what you'd find?"

She slowly nodded, still staring out the window.

"So you're giving up on life? You're giving up a chance at happiness? Don't you think you ought to show a little more courage than that?"

They'd reached her apartment by now. She turned to glare at him, tragedy on her face. Then she opened the car door and ran for her apartment.

"Claire! Wait! I didn't mean—" He got to her door about ten seconds after she'd slammed it shut. "Claire," he called through the door. "I'm sorry. I wanted to force you to think, to fight for our future. I didn't mean to hurt you!"

No answer. He'd blown it. Tomorrow

morning he'd call her. Maybe she would have forgiven him by then.

CLAIRE FINALLY stopped sobbing and sat up on her bed. Why had she cried so bitterly? Was it because he'd made her feel like a coward?

As if probing a wound, she examined her reaction to that suggestion. She wasn't happy that he thought her a coward, but it didn't bring tears to her eyes.

The only other possibility was that he'd stumbled upon the truth she tried to hide from. She'd never allowed herself to get serious about a man because she didn't deserve happiness. Or she was afraid she'd fail another child? Both ideas filled her with panic.

With Tom, she'd fallen in love so quickly, she hadn't realized she was there until it was too late.

Tom's question about why she hadn't looked for her son was difficult, too. She didn't know how to begin, she said, excusing herself. But now that she was aware of what she'd been doing, she wouldn't accept that excuse.

She'd have to begin with her mother. Her father had died six years ago. But her mother might know who had adopted her child. She'd never asked.

She checked her watch. It was only a few minutes until ten o'clock. Her mother usually went to bed just after the news at ten. She picked up the receiver and began dialing the number. Her fingers were trembling and her breathing was too shallow.

"Mom?" she said when her mother answered.

"Claire? Is something wrong?"

"Yes, Mom. I'm okay, but I want to—I want to know who adopted my little boy."

Her mother didn't say anything.

"Mom, I know you and Dad made the arrangements. You may not be able to give me at lot of information, but you've got to have something."

"Why are you asking?" her mother asked, her voice wavery.

"Because I need to know. I should've asked much earlier, but I was afraid to find out. But it's time I face the truth."

"Your father said—"

"Mom, Dad's gone. I know he tried to do

what he thought best for me," she said, almost gagging at that truth, "but he's not here. And I need to know. Before I ruin the rest of my life."

"I'll have to get the papers. Do you want me to hang up so you don't have to pay while I dig them out?"

"No, Mom. I want to wait right here while you look."

She heard her mother laying down the receiver and then her footsteps fading as she left the phone. Just like that, Claire thought. All this time, because she had been afraid, she'd denied herself her son's location. But what if he was miserable? What if he'd been abused? Would she be able to help him? Could she face such a thing?

Faster than she'd hoped, her mother picked up the receiver again. "Hello?"

"I'm here, Mom."

"Mr. and Mrs. Richard Browning adopted him."

"Where do they live?"

"In Austin. They sent pictures and a report every year."

"And you never told me?" Claire demanded, almost screaming.

"I never even saw them. The lawyer in charge of the adoption received and kept the reports—it was one of the stipulations of the adoption agency that the reports be sent out yearly. Your father said not to read them because he thought it would be too upsetting. Better leave things as they were—in the past. Why bring up bad times?"

Claire had never questioned her parents' motives when she was younger. Her father's word was law around their house, and to question him could only mean trouble. So Claire quickly learned to follow his wishes, without hesitation. It was only recently that Claire began to realize just how controlling her dad had been—and how it had affected her life. But now, at thirty, Claire was no longer willing to blindly obey.

"Mom, I just think it's time to start taking control of my life and actions."

Claire paused. Then she said, "Do you have their address or their phone number?"

Her mother gave her both pieces of information, much to Claire's surprise.

"I—I need to go, Mom, but—thank you for giving me this information. I'll call you soon." Once she'd gotten over the unintentional cruelty. Her mother had always been guided by her husband's rules and opinions. It's a wonder she'd given her the information.

She sat down on her bed and stared at the paper she'd written on. Now what? Did she just call them, out of the blue, and demand to see her son?

"No," she answered aloud. She needed an intermediary. Someone to find out how her son was before— So she could prepare herself. Someone to negotiate the possibility of her seeing him, maybe even becoming a part of his life.

Who could she get?

Tom Blake, of course. The best lawyer in Austin for family problems.

Without giving herself time to think, she dialed his number. He answered right away. "Claire? Thank God. I thought you'd never speak to me again."

"This isn't a personal call," she said stiffly.

After a silence that grated on her nerves, he said, "Why else would you call me?"

"I want to hire you."

"To do what?"

"I—I found the name and address of the

couple who adopted my son. I need someone to talk to them, to find out how he's doing. To ask them if I can meet him. Would you— I'll pay for your services.''

Again he hesitated, but, much to her relief, he said, ''Yes, I'll do that for you. Give me the information.''

She did so. Then she asked, ''When— when do you think you'll be able to—to handle this business?'' She tried to keep her voice steady, but she hadn't succeeded.

''I'll call first thing in the morning. It may take a while to set up a meeting, but I'll let you know.''

''Okay, thank you. I'm sorry I disturbed you so late for business, but I—I couldn't wait.''

''It's not a problem, sweetheart. Will you be able to sleep?''

''Of course,'' she assured him, knowing she was lying.

''Good night, then.''

CHAPTER FIVE

AFTER HANDLING only the most pressing things on his desk the next morning, Tom picked up the phone and dialed the number Claire had given him. His heart was beating rapidly as he considered how important this call was. If Claire had believed his theory and could accept happiness, maybe their romance had a chance.

Mrs. Browning answered the phone and Tom quickly explained that he was calling on behalf of her son's birth mother. After she listened to his explanation, the woman invited him to their home at noon, when her husband would be there and they could discuss his proposition.

The rest of the morning was wasted as far as Tom was concerned. He so badly wanted things to work out for Claire. When it neared twelve o'clock, he drove the few miles away to a pleasant, upscale neighborhood where the Brownings lived.

"Come in, Mr. Blake," the woman who opened the door said.

She led him into a dining room where a man stood at once, introducing himself as Richard Browning.

Mrs. Browning invited him to sit down and offered him a cup of coffee. There were cold cuts and fresh bread on the table, along with condiments.

"Please fix yourself something to eat. We don't want you to sacrifice lunch for our convenience," she explained with a smile.

As soon as Tom began doing so, Mr. Browning said, "What we don't understand, Mr. Blake, is why the birth mother is in any doubt about Jordan's situation. We've been sending yearly reports ever since he was born."

Tom stared at the man, surprised. "I beg your pardon?"

"You didn't know?" Mrs. Browning asked.

"No. Claire hasn't known where her son was located or what his situation was. Did you send the reports to her parents?"

"We sent them to our attorney who arranged the adoption. A couple of times we even suggested a possible meeting between Jordan and his birth mother because he had questions. There was never any response."

Tom sighed. "I think Claire would've loved to visit with the boy. She was fifteen when he was born and her parents gave her no choice about adoption. She's worried about him ever since."

"Oh, the poor thing. Of course, we'd be glad for her to visit with Jordan."

Tom reached out and patted the woman's hand. The couple was being very receptive. "You don't have to worry, Mrs. Browning. Claire is a respectable citizen. She's a nurse at Maitland Maternity specializing in preemie care."

"Oh, how wonderful!"

"So, how shall we set this up?" Mr. Browning asked. "I'd like to be here, too."

"How about we come this evening or tomorrow evening for a get-to-know-you visit?"

"It will need to be tomorrow evening because Jordan has a basketball game tonight," Mrs. Browning said. "He plays on the freshman team at school.

"He's tall, then?"

"Fairly," Mr. Browning said with a chuckle. "But he's got a huge heart and lots of determination."

He sounded a lot like his mother, Tom decided.

CLAIRE DISCOVERED Tom waiting by her car when she left the hospital that afternoon. "Hi! What are you doing here?"

"Waiting for you, of course."

"Don't you ever work? Lawyers aren't supposed to finish work at four-thirty. It's still daylight." She'd had friends who were married to lawyers and they always complained about never seeing their husbands. She kept staring at him, though, wondering if he was here because of her phone call last night.

"We're not night creatures, afraid to be seen in the sunlight, I promise. Besides, I have flexible hours."

"I guess you do, since you're the boss," she said. "Did—did you make that phone call?"

"Yeah. How about I tell you everything over dinner?"

"No. Just—just tell me now."

She was tied up in knots. "Your son is fine, and his parents are willing for you to come see him. They've been sending reports to the lawyer once a year and have even suggested you come visit."

Her eyes filled with tears and she closed them, hoping Tom wouldn't notice. But her hands were shaking; in fact, her entire body was shaking. "They don't mind?"

He shook his head.

"Did you see him?"

"No. He was at school."

"When? When can I see him?"

"Tomorrow evening. We can't go tonight because he's playing in a junior varsity basketball game."

"Basketball? He's tall?"

"His dad said he's kind of tall, but mostly he's got a big heart and a lot of determination."

"I—I'm so glad he's happy."

Tom put his arms around her. "You do want to meet him, don't you?"

"Oh, yes, with all my heart," she exclaimed. "Oh, Tom, thank you. Thank you so much. They don't mind? You're sure?"

"I'm sure," he said, smiling now. "They seem like nice people. There were a lot of pictures of the three of them. The house is nice, the mother the kind anyone would love. When Mr. Browning spoke about the boy, there was pride and love on his face. I'd say your son got lucky."

"So did I," she whispered, tears filling her eyes again.

He took her face between his hands. "Hey, no more tears. Things are turning out well."

"Yes, but I could've found him years ago if I hadn't been a coward! If I'd stood up to my dad." She pulled away from him. "You were right. I was a coward. He probably won't want to know me!"

"Lord have mercy, woman! It's time to rejoice, not beat yourself up over what you couldn't control. You were only fifteen! The age he is now. Come on. You did the best you could."

She shrugged her shoulders and laid her head on his.

"Would you like to come home with me

now? Mrs. Dee wondered if you'd do some taste tests tonight.''

"No! No, I couldn't face anyone tonight. I—I don't think I should help with the party!''

"You promised. Besides, it's possible we'll have the way cleared for that wedding I'm interested in.''

"Tom, I can't promise— Your theory was interesting, of course, but I had good reason for breaking up with the men in my life. I'm sure it wasn't—''

"But you don't have a good reason for breaking up with me.''

She stared at him, unable to think of anything.

"See? Come with me tonight. It will take your mind off tomorrow night, so you won't be a nervous wreck. You can help Mrs. Dee by giving your opinion about the hors d'oeuvres. She's counting on you.''

"But—''

"It'll just be you and me tonight. No expectations. If you want to walk away after this weekend, I won't tie you up and hold you captive. Even though I'd like to,'' he assured her with a grin. "Tonight it's just friends."

"I can't—I might not be able to—I'm already nervous."

"I know. This way I can be sure you eat a good dinner and relax just a little. Humor me. I'll knock ten per cent off your bill."

While he was talking, he took her arm and led her to his car. She could've protested, gotten away, gone home. But she wasn't sure she wanted to. This momentous event that would occur tomorrow night would drive her crazy with stress. Maybe if she went with Tom and pretended everything was normal, like it was last week before she decided to stop dating Tom, she would be able to deal with her nerves.

Tom talked her into leaving her car there and they drove to his family home together. Again its beauty was overwhelming, but in no time she was settled comfortably at the breakfast bar on a stool.

Mrs. Dee showed her three recipes she'd tried out that afternoon. She seemed to enjoy talking over the advantages of each one and Claire certainly did, too. She wasn't that great a cook and her mother hadn't encouraged her participation in meal preparation when she was growing up. Instead her mom had wanted her kitchen to herself. She didn't like messes—and children were often messy.

"Tom, try this one," Claire said, calling him to her side. "It's my favorite."

"Then, it's my favorite, too," he immediately announced without tasting it.

"I'm serious," Claire urged.

He opened his mouth and let her pop in a small ham-and-cheese swirl that had a tangy taste. He chewed then smiled. "See, I told you it was my favorite."

"We both like this one, Mrs. Dee," Claire said with a smile. Then she swatted Tom's hand as he reached for another. "You haven't tried the others yet. No doubling up."

"She's so strict," Tom complained, making a face.

"You two and your teasing," Mrs. Dee said with a laugh. "The beauty of this one," she added, pointing to the ham-and-cheese swirl, "is that it can be made ahead of time. And it's easy to make."

"But it looks so complicated," Claire exclaimed.

Mrs. Dee showed her the steps and Claire was impressed. "Wow, even I can do that." She suddenly looked at Tom. "I was thinking of taking tomorrow and Friday off, if I could be of any help, Mrs. Dee. We could make these tomorrow morning, put them in the fridge and be finished with them in no time."

"Good idea," Tom agreed. "Staying busy is a good thing."

"Right," Mrs. Dee agreed with a smile. "And the brisket and smoked turkey will be delivered Friday afternoon, all prepared. All we have to do is put it on the minibuns and heat them. I made arrangements this morning." The housekeeper moved another plate closer. "Try this."

Tom picked up a cracker with cheese and a piece of pepperoni on it. He took a bite, then shrugged. Claire also tasted it.

"That's what I thought," Mrs. Dee said with a nod. "Nothing special." She wrote something on a clipboard. "We won't bother with those then. Besides, with cheese and cracker trays, chips and dips and dessert trays, I think we'll have more than enough.''

"I know you're doing all the work, Mrs. Dee, but it's a lot of fun for me. Thanks for including me," Claire said with a smile.

"Thanks for taking part, Claire. Suzanne and Diane used to, but they're too busy now and it helps to have someone else's opinion—and extra hands on Friday afternoon. The last-minute jobs can get overwhelming." Mrs. Dee began putting things away. "Ready for dinner?"

Tom nodded. "Yeah, but we'll eat here with you."

"But I fixed a nice table in the dining room just for the two of you," the housekeeper said.

"I'm sure it's lovely," Claire said, "but I'd rather eat in here, too. I love this kitchen."

"Well, it is a nice kitchen. So sunny with that big window," she added, waving toward where the table stood, bathed in late-afternoon sunlight. "Okay, if that's what you want, then you two go bring the dishes back in here and I'll serve up."

Being included in the preparations made Claire feel like part of the family. She loved it. "Mrs. Dee is wonderful," she whispered to Tom as they gathered the dishes from the dining room.

He grinned at her. "I told you she was. So I guess you don't have any objection to her working for us?"

"You said just friends tonight. No pressure."

"Sorry. I meant, should we ever decide to marry and move into this house, would you object to Mrs. Dee?"

"No one could possibly object to her. But, should you someday marry, you couldn't possibly need that much help, even if you were serious about this house. Even though it's huge."

"So we'd have a few bedrooms we didn't need. You never know. We may fill them all with kids," he suggested with a smile. "And we might have a lot of overnight guests."

Claire followed him back into the kitchen, and then excused herself so she could wash up before dinner, her mind spinning.

Once they were eating dinner—a chicken

casserole with a garden salad and hot rolls that melted in your mouth—Mrs. Dee asked a question that puzzled Claire.

"So, have you bought a new dress for Friday night?"

Claire looked up, surprised. "What? Me? Why, no. I'm not one of the guests."

Tom smiled. "No, you're not. Mrs. Dee and I had a little chat while you were in the washroom, and we both agree that you would make a fabulous hostess for the party Friday night. And we seem to have overlooked that one minor detail."

"The hostess? No, I'm helping out Mrs. Dee. That's all," she said, a note of panic in her voice. "You said you needed help planning it. That's all."

"You'll be great, Claire!"

"Tom Blake, you are incorrigible!"

"I can take that as a yes then, Claire?"

Claire hesitated, unsure what to do. It might be fun and it would help take her mind off things. She'd have to get a few pointers from Mrs. Dee....

"Okay, I'm in. But next time, make your intentions a little clearer from the start!"

"You'll need to be dressed in a cocktail dress or—or whatever women wear to these things."

She had one tired black dress that would do, but she'd come to hate it, as she'd worn it many times in the past few years.

"A woman deserves a new dress for these events, anyway," Mrs. Dee said. "Tom can take you shopping this evening. There's plenty of time."

"I'd be delighted to do so," Tom assured her, happy again.

"I think something blue to match her eyes and show off her pretty blond hair would be nice."

"Perfect. You have a great eye, Mrs. Dee," Tom agreed.

Claire stared at the two of them. Then she turned to Tom. "You said no pressure!"

"You're right. But it would keep you occupied if we go look around, Claire. You might find something you like. It can be part of your Christmas present," Tom suggested.

"No! You're not going to buy my clothes!"

They had a lively discussion on that topic

until they'd finished eating. Claire stood to help clear the table.

"Now, you two go on," Mrs. Dee ordered. "I'll have this cleaned up in no time, and you've got your shopping to do."

Claire didn't know what to do, but Tom didn't share her indecision. He kissed Mrs. Dee on the cheek, thanked her for dinner and led Claire out to his car.

"Stop looking like I'm going to torture you. We're just going to look at a few dresses," Tom teased.

She didn't say anything. She was pretty sure they'd be shopping in stores she didn't normally enter. Thank goodness she had a credit card. But it wasn't how she'd intended to spend her savings.

Of course, after Tom's news, she'd have probably sat in a corner worrying about tomorrow. Maybe he was right. It wouldn't hurt to look.

Once they'd entered the Christmas crowds, they were swept up into a buying mania. Tom suggested several silly gifts for his sisters, a tiger-striped sweater for Diane that Claire definitely dismissed, and a

Mommy shirt for Suzanne. Claire stared at that, then questioned Tom. "Are you sure that's a good idea? Is she happy about becoming a mommy overnight?"

Tom laughed. "Much to my surprise, she is!"

"I'm not sure. It seems a little pushy."

"Okay," Tom agreed, still chuckling. "Come on, let's find the dress department."

As expected, Tom's suggestions were very expensive, but she enjoyed trying them on. When she found one dress—a royal blue as Mrs. Dee had asked for—it made her feel like a princess and she couldn't resist. "This is the one," she said to Tom as she twirled around in front of him. "It would be perfect for a lot of different occasions. I'd get many uses out of it. I don't even feel guilty buying it."

"You are so right. That one's perfect." He gave her a brief kiss. "Go get changed."

As she returned to the dressing room, the saleslady said, "Your husband is wonderful. Some of them are such grumps when it comes to buying their wives pretty dresses."

Claire started to correct her but decided

not to bother. Besides, even if Tom wasn't her husband, he was definitely wonderful. Which, as he'd said, was the reason she thought she shouldn't marry him.

Oh, well, she decided with a sigh. She'd enjoy it tonight. After this weekend, she'd have to look at her life and make some decisions.

She came out of the dressing room back in her own clothes, carrying the dress she'd chosen. The saleslady reached for it, hanging it on a nearby stand and putting it in a plastic bag.

"What a lovely choice. I hope you enjoy it." She handed the bagged dress over to Claire with a smile.

Claire stared at her. "But you haven't rung it up yet. Here's my card."

"Oh, I used your husband's card, Mrs. Blake. It's all taken care of."

"Come on, honey, people are waiting," Tom said, tugging on her arm.

"But—" she began to protest. But a crowded store was no place to argue over finances. She followed him to his car. Then she dug in her heels.

"That was unfair!" she snapped, having let her anger build while they navigated the crowds.

Tom opened her car door and turned to look at her. "No, what would've been unfair would be for you to spend your hard-earned money, more than you usually spend, on a dress for my benefit."

"But if I buy the dress I'll wear it other places. There's no reason for you to pay for it."

Tom shook his head, a rueful look on his face. "Okay, fine. I'll tack its cost onto my bill. Now let's go home. I'm tired."

She nodded and got into the car. He was right. It was late. She'd had a long day. "Just drop me by the hospital and you'll be home in no time."

"I'll follow you home."

She knew better than to argue. He was very protective. With a sigh, she nodded and got out of his car when they reached the hospital. Once she was in her own, she drove out of the parking lot, Tom right behind her. At home, she unlocked the door to her apartment and waited for Tom to get there.

"Thank you for keeping me busy tonight. You were right. I would've worried myself to death."

"Are you going to be able to sleep now?"

"I'm sure I will. I'm tired." She knew she was lying, but she hoped he didn't.

"Call me if you can't sleep."

CHAPTER SIX

TOM WAS EDGY the next morning. By nine o'clock, he couldn't seem to do much but stare at the telephone, waiting for it to ring. Finally he called his father's house. "Mrs. Dee, have you heard from Claire?"

"Why, yes, she called a few minutes ago. Asked if it would be all right if she got here about ten to help me make those hors d'oeuvres we looked at yesterday."

"Great. How about I join you for lunch. Can you handle that?"

"Of course. I'm sure Claire would like that."

"Okay. Thanks."

He hung up and tried Claire's apartment. No answer. After listening to the answering machine, he left a message for her to call him. He didn't think she would. He was pretty sure she was still there, worrying about tonight.

He shouldn't have left her alone. He was sure she hadn't slept at all. She had to resolve some issues with her son before she could make a decision about Tom. He figured he was as nervous as she. He certainly hadn't slept a lot last night.

Tom had never found a woman he couldn't live without, until he met Claire. He'd do whatever he could for her. In return, all he wanted to do was share his life with her. If he could convince her.

"Mr. Blake? Mr. Michaelson's attorney is on line two," Carol announced, interrupting his thoughts. He didn't want to deal with other people's problems right now, but he couldn't put life on hold. At least he would see Claire at lunch.

He'd hoped to get away by eleven for an early lunch, but he got mired down in negotiations. It was almost noon when he grabbed his briefcase and ran past Carol's desk. "I'll be at my father's house," he said, not stopping in case she tried to slow him down.

Eagerness bubbled up in him as he got closer to the house. He hoped she'd been thinking about him, and happy about the prospects of meeting her son. Most of all, he hoped she'd let him hold her.

He entered quietly and stood at the door to the kitchen, watching her before she realized he was there. She looked tired, worried, but she was wearing an apron and doing as Mrs. Dee suggested.

"Well, looks like this kitchen has a surfeit of great chefs this morning," he said, keeping his eye on Claire.

She jerked the knife away from the ham and cheese and stared at him in surprise. "What are you doing here?"

Mrs. Dee winked at Tom. "Oh, did I forget to mention that Tom was joining us for lunch? We're so close to his office, he likes to do that some days."

"No, you d-didn't say—I mean, of course, he—I don't want to be in the way."

"Don't be silly," Mrs. Dee said. "We're having leftover casserole from last night. You did like it, didn't you?"

Tom grinned. Mrs. Dee was good. Now she had Claire worrying she'd offended the housekeeper instead of thinking about how to get away from him.

As Claire assured her she loved the casserole, Mrs. Dee was taking a pan out of the oven and asking Claire's help in setting the table.

"I'm going to go wash up," Tom said, knowing Claire was in good hands. "Be right back."

When he reached the table, Claire was sitting in the chair she'd occupied last night. "I'm not sure I'll be able to eat anything, Mrs. Dee. I've sampled so much this morning. Those little quiches were a great breakfast. And the cheesecakes! They're heavenly."

"Thank you," Mrs. Dee said as she joined her at the table, the same time Tom sat down. "We've gotten so much done this morning. You're great to work with, Claire. You don't make a fuss about things."

"You two ladies seem to work well together," Tom said, smiling at both of them. But he took Claire's hand in his and squeezed it. "How you doing this morning?"

"Fine," she said, demanding her hand back, her voice clipped.

Tom let it go. First he wanted her to eat. A few minutes later, when they'd finished, he asked Mrs. Dee to excuse them. Claire protested, but he took her hand and tugged her after him. They went to a door under the main staircase.

"This was my mother's favorite room," he announced, catching Claire's attention. It was a warm room, comfy. His mother had done it in chintz, a big stuffed sofa and chairs, a charming desk over by the window.

"I love it!" Claire exclaimed, moving into the room without any prodding from Tom. "It's— You must miss her very much."

"Yeah. Come sit down. I have some things I need to tell you."

Immediately she froze.

"Come on, Claire, it's nothing bad."

With great reluctance, she followed him to the sofa. He looped his arm on the back of the sofa, but she kept her distance.

"When I talked to Jordan's parents last—"

"Jordan? His name is Jordan?" Claire's eyes were wide and she leaned toward him.

"Yes, that's the name they gave him."

"I've wanted to know his name for so long. I didn't even know his name. Any stranger would be given that, and yet I didn't know." Tears filled her eyes.

"Oh, sweetheart," Tom whispered, pulling her into his embrace. "I'm sorry. I think I understand how difficult this is for you, and then I trip up on something like that."

She wiped her eyes and sniffed. "I should've asked sooner, but it's all happening so fast. I can't believe I forgot to ask about his name! I'm being ridiculous, I know, but—"

"You're being a sweet, caring person, as usual."

"I guess," she said, frowning. "I've worried all night. It's possible he may not like me."

He hugged her close again. "What's not to like? You're bright, beautiful and loving."

She shivered and, in spite of telling herself she shouldn't rely on Tom's strength, she buried her face in his neck.

"We'll go over after dinner this evening. Everything will be fine."

She nodded but didn't look at him, afraid he'd see her fears in her eyes. They'd kept her up most of the night.

Her eyes began to close and she caught herself, trying to sit upright so she'd stay awake.

Tom kept her in place. "Just relax for a few minutes, sweetheart. It's going to be a long day."

That made sense, so she let her eyes close. Just for a few minutes.

When Tom felt Claire's body relax against his, he gently eased himself out from under her, slipping several pillows under her head. Then he took the throw from the back of the sofa and draped it over her.

He suspected she'd gotten little sleep last night. He'd known the meeting would be traumatic, but he hadn't really understood how much until she reacted to knowing the boy's name.

If the evening didn't go well, he knew Claire would be devastated.

Back in the kitchen, he explained where Claire was. "I don't think she got much sleep last night."

"Is something wrong? She seemed nervous this morning, but I thought maybe it was working with me. She's such a delight.

I tried to make her feel at home," Mrs. Dee said, a frown on her face.

"No, it wasn't you. I'd tell you, but it's Claire's business. I've already butted in enough. Now, where's one of those cheesecakes? I don't want to be done out of my dessert."

After tasting several desserts he checked on Claire again before returning to the office. She was curled up on the sofa, sleeping peacefully. With a sigh, he refrained from touching her, but it was hard.

Then he stepped back into the kitchen. "She's still sleeping. Don't let her leave here. Tell her I'm coming here to meet her." He realized he'd forgotten something else. "Um, I forgot to tell you we were joining you and Dad, if he's going to be here, for dinner again."

Mrs. Dee smiled. "You know you're always welcome."

"Bless you. I promise we won't eat here every evening.

"Keep Claire here and call me at the office if there's any trouble."

"Will do!"

When he returned from the office four

hours later, there had been no calls from the house. Several times he'd started to call, but he decided he'd be hovering if he did.

So he parked in front and rang the front doorbell. He hoped Mrs. Dee sent Claire to answer it. It would give him some privacy for a hello kiss that he'd been hungering for for several hours.

The scenario played out perfectly and he swept Claire into his arms and lowered his lips to hers. She was trying to say something, but he ignored her.

"Come on in, son," his father's booming voice interrupted the kiss.

He released Claire and looked up. His father and Megan Maitland were standing in the entryway to the living room.

"Hi, Tom, hope we're not intruding," Megan said, chuckling.

Tom wrapped an arm around Claire and moved toward them. "Hi, Megan, Dad. I didn't know you'd be here."

Hugh Blake smiled. "Well, it is my house right now. I usually eat dinner here. And I snuck Meg away from her family for tonight. I hear you and Claire are joining us."

"Yes, if you don't mind. We won't be

hanging around. We've got an appointment later, but it's easier to eat here than to go out.''

''You're right,'' Megan agreed. ''The restaurants are so crowded these days. In fact, all of Austin is crowded. Of course, it's good for business, but it makes it difficult to get around. By the way, we were just admiring your Christmas tree.''

They'd reached the living room where the sparkling tree, its lights turned on, dominated the room. ''Yeah, thanks. We had a lot of fun decorating it, didn't we, honey?''

Claire had said nothing since he'd arrived and the frozen look on her face worried him.

''Yes,'' she whispered.

The four of them sat down and Hugh offered Tom a glass of wine. He refused.

So did Claire. But Mrs. Dee brought her some Diet Cola. ''You want something from the kitchen, too?'' Mrs. Dee asked Tom.

Tom grinned at Claire. ''Diet Cola sounds good. I'll—''

Before he could move, Claire leaped to her feet. ''I'll get it.'' And she ran from the room.

''Claire seems uneasy, Tom,'' Megan said

with a frown. "She's a lovely young woman and a valued employee at the hospital. Is there anything I can do to help?"

"I'm not sure—"

Claire entered the room with a full glass and handed it to him.

"Thanks, Claire."

She sat down beside him, twisting her fingers in her lap, but he noticed they were shaking. "You nervous about tonight?"

With a gasp and a frantic look at the other two, Claire nodded.

"It will be all right," he said, trying to reassure her.

"What's tonight? Something exciting?" Megan asked, a smile on her face.

Claire leaped to her feet again, but Tom grabbed her arm so she couldn't leave. "Thanks for asking Megan, but it's personal."

He pulled Claire back to the sofa and kept his eyes on her. He changed the subject, asking Megan and his dad about their wedding plans, but suddenly, Claire interrupted him.

"I think I should tell them about tonight, Tom. Then we'll know whether they—" She hesitantly turned to Megan. "There's something I'd like to share with you and Mr. Blake.'' Claire paused momentarily. And then with a deep breath, she carried on. ''I had a baby when I was a teenager and gave him up for adoption. I'm going to meet him for the first time tonight.''

CHAPTER SEVEN

CLAIRE STARED at the couple, watching for signs of horror. Not only had she revealed her secret to his father, but also to Megan Maitland, her employer.

Megan's reaction was unexpected. She immediately moved to the sofa where Claire was sitting to take her hand in hers. "Oh, my poor dear. No wonder you're nervous. I thought it was me. I'm sure everything will be all right. However, as it happened, I didn't actually have to go through that stress, since I thought my baby was dead."

Claire stared at her. "You—you really had a baby out of—I mean—"

"Oh, yes. You're definitely not the first to make that mistake," Megan said. "And while I didn't have to prepare to meet my child later, I had to tell my *other* children what I had done." Megan was smiling, so Claire guessed it turned out okay.

"But how—if your child was dead—then—" She couldn't seem to put together a coherent sentence.

"Thank God he wasn't dead. My father lied to me."

Claire gasped again. "My parents lied to me, too."

"Well, they thought they were doing the best thing for you, dear. How old is the child? He can't be too old."

"He's fifteen. I was fifteen when he was born."

"My, you were young. Your parents were probably feeling more guilty for their own behavior than yours. Don't be so nervous. I'm sure things will work out."

"You're being very gracious, Mrs. Maitland...and Mr. Blake. I'm sorry I imposed my problems on you." She didn't look at Tom, sitting on her other side.

Mr. Blake said, "If you're going to become a part of our family, as Tom hopes, Claire, we would meet the boy anyway. Besides, you have nothing to be ashamed about. You made a mistake. You're not the first or last to do so."

Claire blinked her eyes to keep the tears

from falling. "That's more than generous of you, sir. Thank you."

She saw the quizzical look the older man sent his son. He was probably wondering what kind of idiot Tom had gotten involved with. "If you'll excuse me, I need to go— powder my nose before we leave."

"Hurry. We don't want to be late," Tom called.

ONCE THEY WERE IN the car and driving to the Browning house, Claire apologized. "I'm sorry I told your father and Mrs. Maitland about my problems. I know it wasn't polite conversation, but it was all I could think about. And I thought you should know if—if they hated me."

He chuckled. "No, it certainly wasn't normal conversation. But they didn't hate you. I knew they wouldn't."

He pulled to a stop in front of the house and turned to look at her. "We're here."

Claire sat and stared at the lovely home, well-manicured lawn, the nice car in the driveway. "He's not living in poverty, is he?"

"No, not at all. He's very happy, Claire,

I promise. Come on, I'm sure they're waiting for us.''

He got out of the car and came around to help her out, noting her fingers were like ice when he took her hand. He didn't let her go once she was out of the car. ''It's going to be fine, Claire,'' he said reassuringly one more time.

She ignored him.

When they reached the front porch, the door opened before he could press the bell.

''We've been waiting for you,'' Mrs. Browning said, stepping forward to take Tom's hand. Then she turned to Claire and said, ''I'm Margaret Browning. Won't you come in?''

''I'm Claire Goodman,'' Claire managed to say. Tom held her arm to make sure she didn't fall if she fainted. He wasn't sure what her reaction would be.

There were two males standing in the entryway, their gazes fixed on Claire. Tom thought they looked remarkably alike, considering the circumstances. The boy was almost as tall as his dad and had the same clear, direct gaze. But his nervousness showed in his Adam's apple as he tried to swallow.

"This is my husband, Richard, and our son, Jordan." Mrs. Browning didn't add anything else and they all stood in the entryway, not moving.

Tom finally cleared his throat. Claire was devouring the boy with her gaze, as he returned the favor. "Maybe we could go sit down?" Tom asked gently.

"Oh! Oh, yes, of course. Where are my manners? Come in, Miss Goodman. Come sit down. I've made a pot of coffee and there are cookies. Jordan, of course, is drinking milk. We tell him coffee will stunt his growth."

The man chuckled, as if that were a standard family joke, but the boy didn't crack a smile.

Tom clasped Claire's hand in his and pulled her into the family room. He led her to the sofa and they sat. Mrs. Browning sat down beside Claire while her husband and son took the matching chairs at each end.

Silence again.

Tom leaned forward. "We certainly want to thank you for letting us barge into your lives like this. Claire has worried about her son for a number of years.''

''Then why didn't she agree to meet with us when I asked?'' The boy stared at Claire and Tom could see resentment there.

Claire stared at him. ''You—you asked to see me?''

''Two years ago. When Mom and Dad sent in that report as usual, Mom added a note saying I wanted to meet you.''

Claire looked pained and Tom understood why.

''And this year, too. And you didn't even call,'' Jordan added, still glaring at her.

''Son,'' his father said quietly. He didn't add any admonitions and it spoke worlds for their communication that the one word was all he needed for the boy to duck his head and sit back.

''Claire didn't know—'' Tom began, anxious to defend her, but she stopped him.

''Jordan,'' Claire said softly, addressing her son for the first time. ''I didn't learn where you were or anything about the reports until two days ago. That doesn't excuse me because—because it's my fault I didn't know. My parents never mentioned you after I gave birth. None of us spoke about you. I was upset, and somehow I assumed they didn't know where you were. Then, as I got older, I grew afraid to ask questions, fearful that the answers would be—something I didn't want to hear. It was cowardly of me and I have no excuses.''

"I don't believe you,'' the boy said, his words almost sullen.

Mr. Browning leaned forward. "When Jordan wanted more information about you, we put in a note asking that you contact us. He was very disappointed when you didn't.''

"I understand,'' she said keeping her head down. "I should've looked for you sooner.''

Tom looked at the boy. "I think you're being a little hard on Claire. She was only fifteen when you were born. It's a difficult time for any kid.''

Claire lifted her chin and stared at her son. All six feet of him. "All I can do is apologize…and answer any questions you have now.''

"Why should I care now?''

Tom wanted to remind him he was talking to his mother, but Browning got there first.

"Son, either you speak politely to Miss Goodman or don't speak at all. This isn't easy for her."

After staring straight ahead, Claire said, tears streaming down her cheeks, "I didn't look for you because I was afraid you'd hate me for giving you up. Afraid I wouldn't be what you wanted. I—I was f-fifteen and—"

She broke into sobs and Tom couldn't hold back any longer. His arms went around her and she buried her face into his chest.

Tom whispered encouragement to Claire, but already she was pulling herself together. The boy sat in silence, watching her.

Mrs. Browning handed her a tissue, using one herself, and Claire wiped her face. "I apologize. Do you want to ask anything?"

"That was one of them," Jordan said.

"What was?"

"How old you were. Mom and Dad said they thought you were young. Who was my dad?"

"A boy at school," Claire said with a shrug. "I thought he was my one true love," she whispered with an awkward laugh. "My hero. Until he found out what had happened. Then he ran as fast as he could.''

Jordan sounded horrified. ''He didn't stand by you?''

''He was only sixteen, with a bright future, Jordan. Don't blame him.''

''But he left you alone to face everything!''

''Not what we'd consider good behavior,'' Mr. Browning said. ''Jordan has been taught to be responsible for his behavior.''

''I'm glad,'' Claire said, a small smile breaking through. ''I was taught that, too. I gave birth to you, but I never saw you. My father insisted I sign the adoption papers at once and, when they took me home from the hospital, they never spoke of my 'problem' again.''

They all stared at her, incomprehension in their gazes.

''It was a shameful thing, you see. They put me in a new school and pretended I was a carefree teenager.'' She tried to smile again, but it didn't quite make it.

Tom decided it was time to give Claire a break. ''Claire is a nurse at Maitland Maternity Clinic. She takes care of the preemies, the babies who are born too early.''

''Wow, that must be hard,'' Jordan said, looking at Claire with a little more acceptance. Then he asked, ''Have you had other children?''

''No! No, I've never married and—''

''She's going to marry me, I hope.''

Mr. Browning cleared his throat. ''Congratulations. I wish you as much happiness as we've had. Jordan made our marriage perfect.'' He smiled at his son and Tom could see the pride in his gaze. He hoped Claire saw that.

''Would you like to see Jordan's baby pictures, Claire?'' Margaret asked as another uncomfortable silence fell.

Claire looked at Jordan. ''Would you mind?''

''No, I don't mind,'' the boy said, a little surprised by her question.

Soon the two ladies were gathered on the sofa looking at photo albums, with Jordan hanging over the back of the sofa, making comments.

Mr. Browning stood and crossed the room

to stare out a window at the backyard, and Tom joined him.

Without looking at him, the man said, "You know, when Margaret wanted to adopt, I wasn't sure it was such a good idea. I figured without children we could travel, have extra money for whatever we wanted. But I agreed because I loved her.

"Smartest thing I ever did. The past fifteen years have been wonderful. You tell Claire that her sacrifice made a huge difference in our lives. I can tell it was hard on her, but she blessed us."

"I'll tell her. She's had a lot to deal with this week. Are you and your wife going to have any problem with Claire visiting with Jordan occasionally? Like an aunt or something? Letting him visit us?"

"Of course not. We discussed it last night before we went to sleep. The more family Jordan has, the better off he'll be. We still intend to be his parents, but we'd welcome Claire joining the family."

"Good." Tom looked over at Claire and saw the weariness on her face. He decided it was time to cut the evening short. "Claire, do you mind if we go now? I've still got some work to do. Maybe we can make plans to meet soon. When do you play basketball again, Jordan?''

"Next Wednesday. Our games are always on Wednesday afternoons.''

"How about we meet next Wednesday, see the game and we take you and your parents out to dinner?''

"Sure," the boy agreed, sticking his thumbs in his jean pockets. "Uh, I'm no Michael Jordan, you know," he added, shrugging his shoulders.

Claire stood and smiled at him. "You will be to me. Thank you for letting us come— for letting me get to know you and your parents.''

The boy shrugged awkwardly again. "No problem.''

"It's our pleasure," Margaret said softly, behind Claire. Claire turned and, after hesitating, hugged Margaret.

"I appreciate this so much. You've done such a wonderful job of raising him.''

"We thank you for the precious gift you gave us, and I'm sorry it caused you so much pain.''

Tom slipped his arm around Claire and

guided her to the door. "We'll look forward to next Wednesday." Then he led her to the car.

After driving silently for about five minutes, Claire said, "My parents have lied to me by omission for fifteen years."

"Your mother told you the truth when you asked. Maybe they believed you didn't want to know." He cleared his throat. "They may have gone about things the wrong way, Claire, but I think they were trying to do the right thing."

"How terrible to screw up so badly 'trying to do the right thing,'" she said bitterly.

"He's turned out to be a fine young man. And he looks a lot like you."

"Do you think so? I didn't see any resemblance." She stared out the passenger window.

"There's a stubborn line that appears on your face when you're digging in your heels. He has that. There's a generosity of spirit that matches yours, too. And a sense of humor."

After a minute, she said, "The Brownings are very nice…and generous."

"Yes, they are. Mr. Browning told me to

tell you that Jordan has made a huge difference in their lives and he thanks you for him.''

She sniffed several times. ''There's no need to thank me. I didn't do so by choice.''

''Maybe not by choice, Claire, but it was a huge gift, a gift of love that keeps on giving. It's really the spirit of Christmas, only it's for all year round.''

She covered her face with her hands and Tom didn't say anything else until they reached her apartment complex.

''Why don't you go in and gather what you'll need for tomorrow and come back to Dad's house with me?''

''No. No, I need some time to think. I'll be over tomorrow.''

''Will you stay tomorrow night? After the party?'' He grinned. ''Then you don't have to worry about drinking and driving.''

''I don't drink, Tom,'' she said stiffly as she got out of the car.

He followed her, not wanting to end the conversation yet. ''I'd noticed, but I didn't know why.''

''I was drunk the night Jordan was conceived.'' She looked at him. ''I gave up alcohol then.''

''I see. Will you spend the night anyway?''

She hesitated. ''I need time to think. So much has happened.''

''I don't want you to leave me, Claire. Haven't I convinced you of that yet?'' he asked, his heart catching in his chest.

''Tom,'' she began, drawing a deep breath, and he felt sure she was going to completely reject him. ''You were right. My plans to make right giving up Jordan by having another child in a perfect family was childish.'' She closed the car door and leaned against it. ''And I know enough about having babies that there are other ways for us to have children, including adopting.''

He came around the car and took hold of her arms. ''Good.''

''But I have to deal with my cowardice. I'd like to blame everything on my parents, but that would be just as childish. Just give me a little time. I need to get to know the real me.''

He pulled her against him, wrapping his

arms around her. "I know the real you, and you're the one for me. But I'll give you time, if you promise not to run away. To discuss things before it's final."

She laid her head on his chest. "I promise we'll talk. I just can't say when."

"Good enough. I'll see you in the morning at Dad's house. Bring your blue dress."

"Do you still think I should come?"

"More than ever. Until you say no, I'm planning on marrying you. Even if you say no, I can't promise I won't try to change your mind. My world revolves around you."

He kissed her good-night and then left before she could change her mind. At least he still had a chance.

CHAPTER EIGHT

CLAIRE WAS AMAZED when she awoke Friday morning. She'd fallen asleep the night before as soon as she went to bed. She'd expected to lie awake for hours, thinking about Jordan. Instead she'd slept soundly.

This morning, there was a lightness in her step that amazed her. Her child, her son, was happy, well-adjusted, and willing to get to know her. Wednesday night she'd see him again.

And she owed it all to Tom.

He'd held on when she'd tried to say goodbye. He'd forced her to look at herself. He'd been there to help her when she'd asked for help. She didn't have any doubt of his love.

Which made her decision even a little more difficult. She couldn't be selfish and choose to marry him unless she believed she wouldn't hurt him. Tonight was the test.

Last night, Megan Maitland's reaction to Claire's "dirty little secret" took away some of her fears. If Megan didn't have a problem, or Hugh Blake, who else would she worry about?

With hope in her heart, she gathered everything she would need, including her beautiful new gown, and headed to the Blake mansion. Possibly her new home, dare she think it?

She was soon involved with Mrs. Dee, making last-minute preparations. Occasionally, she would sneak into the living room and stare at the beautiful tree. She didn't have a wrapped present for Tom. But she hoped to give him what he'd said was the best gift of all: her love.

When Tom caught her there early in the afternoon, he hugged her and collected a good morning kiss that knocked her socks off.

When he released her, he looked surprised. "Wow. That was very—stimulating, Miss Goodman."

"Yes, it was, wasn't it? Have I thanked you for what you did for me, for Jordan, I mean?" she asked.

"I believe you did."

"Well, I want to thank you again. I realized last night that if you hadn't held on, I might not have realized what I needed to do."

"No problem. I'll add it to your bill."

"Hmm, I'm getting worried about how I'll pay that bill, Mr. Blake. I owe you a great deal."

"Marry a rich lawyer and he'll take care of it." He smiled but she read the seriousness in his gaze.

When she started to speak, he raised his hands and said, "I know, I know, I'm supposed to be patient. How are things going in the kitchen?"

Claire took a deep breath and grabbed Tom by his shirt. She'd done a lot of thinking, too much thinking. She knew what she wanted, and she finally believed she deserved to be happy. And was willing to fight for it, as Tom was.

"I don't want you to be patient."

He froze, staring at her. "You've made up your mind?"

She nodded, wondering how he'd react.

He didn't hesitate. His lips covered hers

and he lifted her in the air, spinning her around as he kissed her deeply. When he finally released her, he asked for more details. "You'll marry me?"

"Yes, please," she agreed, beaming at him.

"Claire, I'm so happy. So pleased. I've never— You're the most wonderful woman in the world. At once? Will you marry me at once?"

She nodded again.

Suddenly, they were no longer alone. His father and Megan Maitland came in the front door, and Diane and Whitney came from the kitchen.

Tom looked at Claire, a question in his eyes.

She nodded again.

"Hey, we're going to be married," he announced loudly so everyone could hear. There was a swell of congratulations. Mrs. Dee stuck her head in the door from the kitchen, a beaming smile on her face.

"Mrs. Dee, did Dad tell you I'm buying the house from him?"

"Why, no! That's wonderful. I wondered what would happen to it."

"It will be fine as long as you stay. Will you, Mrs. Dee? I've asked Claire to marry me, and we're going to need you."

Her face suddenly crumpled and Tom was afraid he'd done something wrong. She covered her face with her apron.

"Mrs. Dee? What's wrong?" he asked, hurrying to her side.

"I—I didn't know. I knew Mr. Blake would be fair, but I love it here."

"You thought you were about to be tossed out on your rear? That was careless of us. Of course that wouldn't happen. And if you want to go with Dad to Megan's house, I'm sure he'll take you. But Claire and I need you."

"I'd love to work for you and Claire. But are you sure? Some newlyweds like to be alone."

"I'm sure Claire will want a family. We'll need you."

"Oh, my, yes! That's wonderful!"

He hugged her. "Everything's wonderful!"

Claire had never felt so welcome, or so happy. The perfect family she'd dreamed of paled in comparison to the love she had for

Tom and his family. The lights on the Christmas tree twinkled on them as she got the best Christmas present of all.

Tom, however, had one more present for her. He pulled her to the sitting room where she'd napped. "I have one thing to tell you. Whitney came to my office today to say she'd let us adopt her babies. Is that okay?"

She couldn't believe her good fortune. "Oh, Tom, that's wonderful. Our family will be complete!"

"We'll see," he said, a twinkle in his eye.

THE ENDS OF THE EARTH

Muriel Jensen

Dear Reader,

I love Christmas! I feel enriched by the spiritual significance, really enjoy the family and community aspects, and I even like the commercial stuff that upsets everyone else.

I love to see ornaments for sale in September, garlands hanging in October and listening to my Christmas carol tapes in November. I'd like to condition myself to shop early, too, but I'm afraid I'll miss something wonderful in the final rush of sales in the middle of December.

So for months I don't do anything productive in preparation for Christmas. I'm not a good cook or skilled at crafts. I just wander around and absorb the atmosphere. I window-shop, hoard holiday magazines, watch all the television specials—it isn't Christmas until I've seen *White Christmas* at least twice. And I plot Christmas books.

Christmas is the perfect romance novel element: families gathering despite their conflicts, food in abundance, children everywhere, and most recently two lonely people hoping to find the world in each other. Add to that Maitland Maternity Clinic "where the luckiest babies are born," and you have everything necessary for a holiday story to put you in a festive mood.

Merry Christmas! And don't forget to linger under the mistletoe!

Muriel Jensen
P.O. Box 1168
Astoria, Oregon 97103

CHAPTER ONE

DIANE BLAKE SAT in a corner of Anna Maitland Cahill's elegant, crowded living room balancing her buffet plate and coffee cup wishing she were somewhere else. On a tropical island, maybe, with scented winds caressing her body. Or on the parapet of a Scottish castle looking down onto the wild Atlantic.

This wedding luncheon was just the kind of social event she dreaded. It wasn't that she disliked people, but that she liked them one at a time, not in large, intimidating groups that made her feel shy and tongue-tied.

As a teacher of social studies at Bluebonnet High, she spoke all day to what everyone else considered a tough audience. But she loved teenagers, and it was a great pleasure for her to teach them about the subject that so excited her, the people and places that populated their world.

She knew her shyness was the result of growing up in a household with a father and two older siblings who knew precisely what they wanted in life, and had the determination and the smarts to get it.

That was how this luncheon came to be. Diane's father, Hugh Blake, a corporate lawyer, fell in love with Megan Maitland, CEO of Austin, Texas's Maitland Maternity Clinic. She was mother, mother-in-law, or grandmother to most of the guests here today. Megan lived a very busy life and had had a million excuses why she didn't have time for a relationship, but Hugh had been determined.

The wedding was scheduled for Christmas Day—a mere six days away.

Diane's siblings, Tom and Suzanne, inherited their father's people-personality and his preference for having things his way. Tom was a partner in a thriving family-law practice. Suzanne founded and managed a fashion accessories house that had made the December cover of *W* this year. A scarf she'd designed was the hit of the retail season with proceeds going to breast cancer research.

Diane, on the other hand, took after their mother, Ellie, a shy, gentle woman who had loved people but hated parties. She'd cooked and gardened and enjoyed reading and needlework—an unapologetic throwback to the fifties woman. The only difference between them was that Ellie had felt rooted in her home and never cared to go anywhere. Diane, however, had been born with wanderlust and preferred travel books to fiction.

So far, she'd been unable to indulge that desire; every time she planned a trip, something came up to prevent her going.

Her trip to Mexico had fallen through when Suzanne broke her leg and Diane spent spring break caring for her.

She'd had to bow out of a cruise to the Mediterranean that she'd planned with two other teachers when her car died of old age and she'd had to buy a new one. Responsibility, she'd thought, required that she use her savings and leave her trust fund untouched.

The trip to Scotland and Ireland she'd planned for last August had been canceled when Whitney Davis, one of her favorite students, had appeared on her doorstep, hysterical. Because of a thinly supervised social life and a charming but irresponsible boyfriend, who'd since moved with his family to another state, she was pregnant.

"Mom threw me out of the house," she'd told Diane tearfully over a cup of cocoa.

"But we talked about this when you first learned you were pregnant," Diane said. "Your mother told you you could stay with her."

Whitney was sixteen, a fresh-faced redhead with yards of hair and a million freckles. She looked as though she should be going to summer camp instead of preparing to become a mother.

Her dark-blue eyes streamed tears. "Yeah. But Wednesday, her boyfriend moved back in, and yesterday..." Her face crumpled again and Diane moved closer to put an arm around her.

"What happened yesterday?" she asked gently.

"My—my ultrasound," Whitney replied. She looked up at Diane with misery in her eyes. "It's twins! And I don't know what to do! Aunt Joyce said she'd take me in, she's moving from a studio apartment into a house, but the deal on it won't close until the end of December.''

Diane had checked with every agency in the county that worked with teens and there was no help for Whitney. All the teen foster homes were overpopulated, and even the shelter for pregnant teens was filled to capacity.

So Diane had temporarily taken in a sixteen-year-old who was pregnant with twins and put off the trip to Scotland and Ireland.

AT THE MOMENT, Whitney sat across the room with her crystal buffet plate perched dangerously on the edge of her knees since she no longer had a lap. Sitting beside her was Beth Redstone, one of Megan's daughters. She had a four-month-old and Whitney was laughing as the baby gave her a gummy smile.

A light flashed on them. Diane turned her head in annoyance, and found Anna's photographer who'd been the bane of her existence the past two weeks, focusing on the charming tableau.

Without thinking twice, she placed her plate and cup carefully on the low table before her and wound her way through chatting knots of people to reach the photographer.

Without looking away from the scene he focused on through the viewfinder, he stopped Diane with one hand upraised to hold her off several feet away.

"Almost got it," he said, his attention on his task. "Just need a grin from the baby—come on, come on—there!" The camera whirred and flashed several times. Then he lowered it and turned to her with the knowing look that had irritated her since she'd met him. He was tall and fit in dark-brown slacks and jacket over a turtleneck that was just a shade lighter. He had dark hair cut short and clear blue eyes that seemed to look through her. He made her nervous in a way that had nothing to do with her customary shyness. She hated that. It made her feel more inadequate than she already did.

"Miss Blake," he said, slinging the camera over his shoulder. He caught her arm and drew her with him toward the buffet table. "How are you today—besides angry? Every

time I see you, there's murder in your eyes.
That must be exhausting. Champagne?''

Without waiting for her answer, he poured
her a glass and handed it to her.

She took it because she didn't want to
make a scene in her soon-to-be stepsister's
home.

''I asked you to stop photographing Whitney,'' she said

''No, you asked me to stop photographing
you.'' He chose a toothpicked hors
d'oeuvres from one of the many plates on
the table and handed it to her. ''And I
haven't even come near you tonight.''

She pushed his hand away and he popped
the little square of stuffed phyllo into his
mouth.

''I think that's what's bothering you.'' He
made another selection—this one a shrimp
skewered with a twist of red pepper. He offered it to her.

She ignored it. A lineup of guests was filling their plates on the other side of the table.
''What do you mean?'' she demanded quietly so they wouldn't hear her.

He picked up a small plate of chocolates
and held it for her to make a choice. ''Have

one. Chocolate has mood-elevating properties.''

"I do not need mood elevating! I just need to be left alone!"

"*That* was my point." He put the plate down again, then led the way across the room to a quiet corner on the other side of a large fireplace.

Diane told herself she followed him only because she didn't get his point, and she wanted to in order to fight back.

"Your family loves you but doesn't really consider you a force within their group, and you're doing your best to hide from the Maitlands because they're all bright and successful and you don't want to be held up in comparison. Why is that? Why do you strive to blend into the wallpaper?"

She gasped in indignation. "I teach high school," she reminded him. "You cannot reach teenagers by blending into the wallpaper."

He nodded, claiming one half of a mission-style settee and urging her down onto the other half. "That's right. You're different around children. Are you more comfortable with them?"

"As a matter of fact, I am," she replied, bristling as she sat stiffly beside him. "But what business is that of yours?"

He smiled in the face of her hostility. "Because a photographer doesn't just freeze the moment and walk away. It's as though every photo taken becomes a permanent part of me. And I want to understand what I'm carrying around."

She was startled by the notion that he might be carrying around images of her in his mind. "You've photographed me all of three times. I'm sure you can forget me."

He shook his head, his expression pleasantly stubborn. "I can't. It's not the same as a memory. It's like…cells or tissue, part of my being. I see a woman with all the qualities that should give her great confidence— beauty, intelligence, a job at which she's very good—" He grinned wickedly. "Nice legs," he added, "and yet you sit shyly in a corner, attracting the children, but hoping none of the adults will speak to you."

She made a face at him. "I suppose you're the kind of photographer who sheds light on a scar or a mole and considers it artful, when your subject probably spent his whole life trying to hide that very thing.''

''Shyness is hardly an ugly scar,'' he corrected. ''But the fact that you think of it that way suggests you consider it something you want to be rid of.''

Diane pointed to her sister, Suzanne, who held court across the room with Dr. Doug McKay, to whom she was engaged. ''Suzanne's very photogenic,'' she said, hoping to divert him. ''Or, there are all these beautiful babies and children running around.'' She pointed as a group of toddlers ran past.

''Diane,'' he said, leaning an elbow on the back of the settee and pinning her with his gaze. ''You aren't under the mistaken impression that my interest is strictly professional, are you?''

HER EXPRESSION was priceless. He'd have liked to focus on her at that very instant. Her eyes were wide with surprise, her pink cheeks deepening in color, her soft mouth startled open. He was good at reading faces—female faces in particular. And as a photographer, he knew that the most interesting details were under the surface of an expression, the telltale hitch in the curve of a mouth that filled a smile with sadness rather than joy, the emotions in the depths of a pair of eyes that belied the exterior calm.

But Diane puzzled him and he guessed that was why he found her so fascinating. Women often hid what they felt, but he guessed she didn't even *know* what she felt. It was as though the pretty, ingenuous woman whose body she wore was completely separate from the longing woman who looked out from her eyes.

And she had no idea what to do with his direct approach. He saw her try to draw coolness around herself like a cloak.

"Please," she said, her tone frosty to match the mood she thought she conveyed. But he saw the warmth in her eyes. "I'm just not a sexual being. I love children and education, and that's absolutely all I—"

He wasn't sure what made him do it. Maybe it was this protracted exposure to the Maitlands, who were all style and good manners, that made him want to be wicked. Or the look in her eyes that said she was attracted while she made every effort to convince him that she could care less. The fortuitous presence of two men engaged in a lively discussion who happened to stop right in front of them as the younger one made a strong point, separated them from the view of the rest of the room. So Jason indulged himself.

He cupped the back of her head in one hand while using the other to secure her chin in the notch between his thumb and forefinger. Then he kissed her firmly, making it clear that he didn't believe her claim for one moment.

Her lips were cool and parted, ripe for his tender explorations.

She put a hand against his chest as though she would push him away and he relaxed his hold on her, willing to allow her her freedom if that was the way it had to be. There was a moment of indecision.

But as he nipped her bottom lip and coaxed her mouth into melding with his, her hand went lax and she seemed to decide the experience might be worth her while after all.

He gave the contact everything he had, confidence mingled with finesse, art taking precedence over impressive performance. He cajoled her with nips and kisses until she responded with an impressive style of her own.

He felt her fingertips on his cheek, his earlobe, in the hair just above the collar of his shirt.

She drew away suddenly, her eyes still wide, but with confusion this time, as though being kissed by him—or perhaps kissing him herself—hadn't been at all what she'd expected.

While he was trying to decide if that was good for him or bad, he became aware of being watched—and not by Diane. She was looking up into the faces of the two men who'd stopped in front of them to pursue their argument, and provided a convenient screen for the kiss.

After two weeks with the Maitlands, Jason knew them well. They were Hugh and Tom Blake—Diane's father and brother.

CHAPTER TWO

HUGH, A TALL, impressive man with a big voice turned to Tom and said, "I thought you told me she wasn't seeing anyone?"

Tom frowned at Diane, then at his father. "That's what she told me."

Jason freed his pink-cheeked companion and got to his feet. "I just took advantage of the moment to prove a point," he said, offering his hand to Hugh. "I'm Jason Morris, the photographer hired by your wedding planner."

Hugh took his hand and, however unconsciously, tried to grind it to powder. "Yes. I know who you are. I remember your press photos of the bombing in Oklahoma City."

At the memory of that photo Jason could feel the horror of those days all over again.

"You won the Pulitzer for that," Tom said.

Jason nodded. "That assignment ended

my career in photojournalism. Death is awful to photograph, but dead children... It is indescribable.'' He drew a breath and pointed to a stream of children running toward the kitchen. ''Seeing loved and healthy children is much easier to take. You're acquiring quite a brood of grandchildren.''

Hugh watched the children with a grin. ''Yes. I like that.'' He refocused his attention on Diane and held a hand down to help her to her feet.

''And what point was Jason trying to make with you?'' he asked.

Diane gave Jason a look that told him he'd pay for this embarrassing moment. ''I think he was trying to convince me that he's irresistible,'' she replied coolly. ''It didn't work.''

''It looked like it was working,'' Tom disputed.

Diane cast him a threatening glare. ''But no one asked you, did they?''

Tom ignored her. ''I volunteer the information,'' he said with an amiable clap on Jason's shoulder, ''because her mind is so occupied with the ends of the earth, that she seldom sees what's right in front of her face.

She's a little thick sometimes. Getting through to her requires considerable and continuous effort.''

DIANE WATCHED Jason and Tom bond over a discussion of her shortcomings. And as though that wasn't bad enough, Suzanne suddenly burst into the group, looping an arm in their father's. "What's going on?" she asked interestedly.

"We're picking on Diane," Tom replied, clearly pleased with that information.

Suzanne smiled widely. "Oh, good. I love a worthwhile cause. What can I contribute? Her weakness is caramel, she's afraid of the dark, she has a life-size cutout of Harrison Ford in her classroom." She delivered those three points brutally and gleefully. "And it is virtually impossible for her to see someone in trouble and fail to offer help. She's the quintessential Good Samaritan, and continues to be even when her efforts go unappreciated and unrewarded." Her eyes narrowed on Diane's. "You look...startled." To Jason, she added, "She's seldom surprised or upset by anything. She's always even-tempered and steady. Did you do something?"

Suzanne had always been direct.

Apparently, so was Jason Morris. "I kissed her," he replied.

Suzanne looked pleased but surprised. "And she didn't slug you?"

"There wasn't time. Your father and brother arrived."

"We didn't slug him," Tom contributed, "because she seemed to be enjoying herself."

"All right, that's enough." Diane asserted herself with her family only on rare occasions. She allowed them their questions and their advice because she appreciated their concern, but sometimes they went too far. "I would appreciate it if you wouldn't leave me out of your discussions about me! Whom I kiss or why is none of your business. Now, if you'll excuse us, Jason and I have things to talk about."

Suzanne looked distressed. "But I have more questions."

Tom took her arm and began to draw her away. "Save them. We'll wait until we can get it out of her without witnesses. Coming, Dad?''

Hugh hung back as Tom and Suzanne started away. He shooed them on. "I'll be right behind you." He looked into Jason's eyes.

Jason met his gaze evenly.

Hugh's eyes went to Diane. "Did he take that kiss, or did you share it?''

The truth was hard to admit to herself, but it was the truth nonetheless. "We shared it," she admitted.

Hugh's eyes swung back to Jason. "She's the most generous woman on earth," he said gravely, "but she's held her emotions very closely. I know that artists sometimes...use others as a way to lend texture to their own lives and their work."

Diane couldn't believe that her father was threatening Jason, however subtly.

"Daddy..." she began.

"I'm a photographer," Jason interrupted. "The art's in the subject, not in me. I have no intention of using your daughter for the enrichment of my work. Although I have to admit that the camera loves her."

Hugh considered that answer and seemed

unable to decide whether or not he believed it. Then he nodded. "Just wanted you to know that I gave my children life, and I figure that gives me the right to bring death to anyone who hurts them."

Diane was surprised when Jason smiled. "I got that message. You have no reason to worry." He extended his hand. "That's a promise."

Hugh took it. "I'll hold you to that," he said.

Diane held both arms out in exasperation. "Will you listen to yourselves?" she demanded under her voice. "You sound like a knight and a dragon bargaining for the life of a lady."

Hugh gave Jason one last, long look. Then he gently pinched Diane's chin. "I'd say that's about right." And he walked away.

Diane turned to Jason and poked him in the chest with her index finger. "See what you've done? My life was just getting to the point where my family wasn't hovering over me, and you had to go and remind my father that I'm the baby of the family, and that there are big bad wolves around!"

He frowned. "I think I liked the dragon analogy better."

"Well, neither one is necessary," she said, "because you're going to leave me alone. I know we're going to keep running into each other at family functions until the wedding, but you are not to photograph me or speak to me, is that clear?"

He arched an eyebrow. "Whoa. I'm not one of your students, so please don't bark orders at me. And if you don't want me to pursue you, you're going to have to give me a reason other than you're not a sexual being, because I think we just disproved that one."

She angled her chin, trying to hold on to her dignity. He *had* shredded that claim. And the really shocking thing was that she'd thought it valid at the time.

"Maybe I just don't want anything to do with you."

He shook his head with pretended regret. "You melted in my arms."

She didn't want to hear that. "Look," she said reasonably. "I have the care of a pregnant teenager, which is going to keep me far too busy for a relationship."

He nodded. "And I'm going to Nouméa for six months after the first of the year. I'm not proposing marriage, I just think you're very beautiful, and as a man whose job it is to find the most interesting subject around him and shine a light on it, I'd like to get to know you."

She heard everything he said, but focused on the one thing that made her feel a surprising sense of— She wasn't even sure what it was. Disappointment? "Nouméa?"

"Yes." He reached to the table for his champagne glass. "I have a contract with Manhattan Publishing to do a coffee table book about the island. It's near New—"

"I know where it is," she interrupted, a little sharply she thought when she heard the tone of her own voice. She softened it deliberately. "It's off New Caledonia. It has plants dating back to the dinosaur age."

He inclined his head with respect for her knowledge. "You do know your stuff. That's precisely what I'm being sent to photograph."

"I've always wanted to go there," she said, wondering what had happened to her indignation over his kiss. He was going away. She felt both relief and regret.

He downed the last of his champagne and replaced the glass on the table. "You're welcome to come with me," he said casually. "I'm sure it'd be good for you, too. Every social studies teacher should have an up-close-and-personal knowledge of the plants of the dinosaur age."

She wasn't sure if he was teasing or not, only that this surprising and annoying attraction was going to have to die right here.

"Or you could meet me there," he added before she could answer, "considering your responsibilities to Whitney, and your contract with the school. There's spring break, summer vacation..."

"Nothing," she said firmly, "can come of this." She knew she was trying to convince herself as well as him.

"You'll never," he said, copying her tone, "convince me of that."

"I don't have to," she said with a dispirited sigh. "I just have to say goodbye."

That dramatic line delivered, she turned to head for Anna's back bedroom and its pile of coats, when she found herself face-to-face with her hostess.

"Here you are!" Anna said, wrapping an arm around Diane's shoulders. "And Jason, too. You're just the pair I wanted to see."

Diane was almost afraid to ask. "Why?"

"Because I'd like Jason to photograph you baking the cookies for the reception favors." She drew Jason into her other arm. He came to her while glancing smugly at Diane.

"I can do that," he said amenably.

"And I'd like you to get pictures of her and my sisters decorating the banquet room for the reception." Anna turned to Diane. "Austin says you can put up all the maps you want."

Anna's husband, Austin Cahill, owned the Austin Palace, one of the Southwest's finest hotels, and had volunteered use of one of its banquet rooms. With Megan and Hugh embarking on a world cruise for their honeymoon, the theme was established, and maps seemed the ideal decoration. Diane had put out the call to everyone in the family for maps of any kind so that she could create a border all the way around the room.

Anna had volunteered her services as wedding planner, but Megan's children, and Diane and her siblings, had been so delighted with the match and their parents' happiness, that they'd wanted to make their contributions to the wedding by doing many of the preparations themselves. So Diane, with her social studies experience, had been put in charge of decorations and the international cookies that would be part of the favors for the wedding guests.

Diane groaned inwardly at the prospect of being forced into contact with Jason Morris at least twice more.

"Is that all right with you, Diane?" Anna asked. "You won't mind having Jason follow you around?"

Diane smiled bravely. "Of course not, Anna," she said. "Whatever you want."

CHAPTER THREE

WHITNEY LOOKED TROUBLED as she cleared away their breakfast dishes the following morning. Diane gathered ingredients for the cookies she'd be making today, a little troubled herself at the prospect of Jason coming by. Ellie Cassidy and Abby McDermott, who'd planned to help, called early this morning to tell her they were stuck at the clinic. Ellie was Maitland Maternity Clinic's administrator, and Abby was an ob-gyn and Whitney's doctor while Doug McKay was away at a conference.

Diane tried to forget her own problems and concentrate on Whitney. "Something wrong?" she asked, coming to the table to hand her her vitamins and a glass of water. She tended to forget them if Diane didn't remind her. "Feeling okay?"

Whitney swallowed the pills, then handed back the glass and nodded, rubbing her stomach. "Yes. I feel a little pressure, but otherwise I'm fine."

"Is something other than the babies bothering you?"

Whitney sank into a chair at the table. Her hair was caught back in a fat, fashionably mussy twist today, and she looked fresh and healthy in an oversize blue shirt and black knit pants.

"Just life in general, I guess," she said with a philosophical sigh. "I—I'm wishing I'd been more careful, that I'd listened to all the cautions, that Brandon had been more adult and more...in love with me."

Diane sat near Whitney and reached for her hand. "There's an unfortunate tendency in most of us to think people don't know what they're talking about when they warn us away from the perils and pitfalls of life. Until we experience it ourselves and realize we should have listened. Then we have to learn by our mistakes—and regrets don't help. You just have to make the best of what is and keep going."

Whitney stared at their hands, eyes unfocused, then sighed and squeezed Diane's fingers. "I know. And I'm so lucky that you're helping me." She seemed to put aside her concerns abruptly, then looked at the clock. "Tom and Claire will be here in five minutes. I'd better get moving."

Whitney had agreed just last week that Diane's brother Tom and his fiancée, Claire Goodman, would adopt her twins. They were going to Tom's partner's office that morning to set up the agreement and a fund for Whitney's education.

Diane held on to Whitney's hand as she would have moved away otherwise. "Tom and Claire will make great parents," she reassured her.

She nodded. "Yes, I know." Then she drew away and went to get her jacket.

Jason arrived with Tom and Claire.

"Look who we found on the elevator," Tom said, pointing to Jason.

They all went into the kitchen, Tom sniffing the air expectantly. "No cookies yet?" Tom asked in disappointment.

"Jason wouldn't be able to photograph the process," Diane said patiently, "if I'd made the cookies already, would he?"

Tom frowned at the lineup of bowls, measuring cups, spoons and ingredients.

"You're making six different kinds. You could have started one. You'll be here all night."

"I'll be here for several days," she corrected.

Claire, rolled her eyes at his behavior. "You'd never guess he just had a Denver omelette and three pieces of toast. Maybe if you promise he can sample cookies when we get back, I can get him out of here."

Tom peered into an empty bowl. "No chocolate chips or nuts or anything that should be tasted before they go into a recipe?"

"I'm ready." Whitney appeared, a plaid poncho draped over her making her look like a decorative little hill. She smiled at Tom. "The twins are going to have the Cookie Monster for a father?"

Diane knew Whitney liked Claire and Tom. Claire and Whitney had talked about the time when Claire had struggled with the emotional trauma of finding the child she'd been forced to put up for adoption years ago. Whitney had sympathized with Tom's infertility and Claire's desire for a baby. That was when Whitney suggested that Tom and

Claire would be the perfect adoptive parents for her twins.

Claire caught Tom's hand and patted it. "I assure you, Whitney, that he's much more mature than he appears when it comes to cookies. Come on, Tom. We don't want to be late."

"Right." He ushered Claire and Whitney through the living room toward the front door. When Diane followed, he turned to stop her with a raised hand. "We'll see ourselves out. Get busy with those cookies. Bye, Jason. Watch yourself with Diane. I don't want to have to kill you."

Jason looked up from his camera with a smiling wave to acknowledge the threat. He grinned at Diane when the door closed behind Tom. "What is this predilection your family has to violence?"

"We have a pirate ancestor," she replied, feeling all the calm in the room evaporating with the closing door. She tried to keep her manner light. "Red Robbie Blake. Robbed and pillaged and charmed the ladies. He was hung at thirty-two. I've always sworn that's where my father gets his skill in banking."

She began to measure ingredients. She felt

him step up behind her, so close that she could feel his breath stir her hair.

Did he really find her as fascinating as he claimed? she wondered breathlessly.

She heard the click of a camera shutter over her shoulder, then the whirr of its inner workings. He wasn't fascinated with her at all, she realized with a sudden sense of annoyance and embarrassment. He was just doing his job!

He came around to her right side and leaned far back into the corner of the counter as she broke egg whites into a bowl.

"I can't believe Megan and my father will find photos of egg whites interesting." She fit the bowl under the beaters of her tabletop mixer.

"Maybe someday," he said, closing in several feet, "you'll want to do a cookbook on cookies from around the world and we'll have a head start with these photographs."

She made a face that disparaged the idea, then turned on the beaters. The next five minutes or so were too noisy for conversation. She beat the egg whites, then, after soft peaks formed, she raised the speed and gradually added the sugar until the soft peaks stood straight. She turned off the beaters.

"That look must have meant that you have no plans for a cookbook," he said, as though their conversation had not been interrupted. He came closer to shoot right into the bowl.

She began to fold in half the flour.

"No, I haven't." She concentrated on her work, treating the mixture gently. She wanted these French *tuiles* to be perfect. "It's just teaching and travel in my future—and the travel has to wait until Whitney's settled in with her aunt. That's supposed to be right after Christmas, but I'm not depending on it. When I make plans, fate has a way of changing them."

Diane stirred in the butter mixture, then folded in the remaining flour while Jason photographed her kitchen.

"Where's your favorite place?" He shot a wooden spoon she'd balanced over the mouth of a bowl, connected measuring spoons dangling from it.

"I want to see Scotland so desperately."

"Mmm. You'll love it. It has atmosphere, weather, mountains, bogs, castles, you name it." He rearranged a copper pot next to a rumpled tea towel and a rolling pin, then took several photos. "Where have you been that you've enjoyed the most?"

"Boston," she replied, trying to make it sound like Addis Ababa. "Back Bay, the Athenaeum, the public library, the view of Harvard across the Charles River."

"Yeah. I like Boston. But I meant your favorite place out of the country."

She finally admitted with a sigh, "I haven't been out of the country."

He lowered the camera to look at her in surprise. "You haven't?"

She smiled sheepishly. "I've never been off the continent." She drew a parchment-covered cookie sheet toward her and began dropping level teaspoonfuls of the batter onto it.

He set the camera on the table, then came back to the counter to lean against it and watch her work. "Why is that?" he asked. "You teach social studies, and you're obviously a lady of means. You talk about exploring the world as though you have to do it or die."

With the back of a spoon, she smoothed

each drop of batter into a small circle. "That's how I feel. But something always comes up." She told him about her thwarted trips. "I couldn't just leave Whitney to fend for herself."

"That was generous of you," he said. "I can't believe the law allows a parent to just turn out a pregnant girl. It's kind of eighteenth century."

"That's what I thought. But there was no place else for her to go." She explained about her aunt's impending move. "And her caseworker tried hard, but there was no social program with room for her."

"Whitney does seem to appreciate you."

"She's fun to have around. I wake up to Britney Spears or 'N Sync blaring from the CD player, and my telephone line is always tied up, but she has a lively personality and it prevents me from getting too serious."

She carried a filled cookie tray to the oven. He opened the door for her, then closed it as she set the timer.

"It wasn't that long ago that you listened to music and talked on the phone for hours, was it?" he asked.

She drew another pan toward her and kept

working. "I loved music, but I was part of the orchestra in school and my taste in music is more classical. And I never talked on the phone. I was always serious about my homework. In my spare time I used to plan trips." She turned to smile at him, feeling herself relax a little and longing to know more about him.

"Tell me about your travels," she pleaded softly. "Where have you been?"

WITH HER SOFT brown eyes glancing his way, clearly hungry for details, he began to talk about his favorite places. He searched his memories for the little things that would make his travels come alive for her.

While she worked he talked about Europe, still his favorite continent despite many trips to more distant and exotic locales. "There's no place like Paris in the morning, London during the business day, or Florence at sunset from the battlements in the hills."

When the cookies came out of the oven, she removed them from the cookie sheet while they were still soft and shaped them on a rolling pin to get the curve of the famous French roof tiles for which they were named.

"That would be my favorite thing to see," she said, touching the cookies as though they were precious jewelry. "The capitals of the world from a hilltop or a church steeple. I love pictures of rooftops. I'd like to see cities the way birds and angels see them."

"Speaking of angels—" he indicated the elegant angel dressed in gold mesh atop the Christmas tree in her living room "—you wouldn't believe Switzerland at Christmas. It's a winter paradise with all the atmosphere you'd ever want."

She smiled. "Okay, that'll be another goal. Switzerland at Christmas."

By lunchtime, she'd made several hundred tuiles and was mixing the dough for *kourabiedes,* a Greek cookie that seemed to require brandy as she asked him to reach into an overhead cupboard for a fat, dark bottle.

"How many cookies do you have to make?" he asked, studying the army of cooling tuiles.

"I figured a couple of hundred of six different kinds."

"You're kidding!"

"We're expecting one hundred and thirty guests, and our combined families is a huge number, so for everyone to have at least one of each cookie, it's going to take that many."

"But, you don't know that everyone will eat one cookie of each kind."

"No, these aren't for the table, they're favors for the guests." She reached to the corner of the counter to hook a floury index finger in a small, simple, two-handled brown bag. A sprig of holly had been tied to the front with a loop of gold ribbon. "I'm going to put them in these. I think two hundred should do it."

He took the bag from her. "Simple chic. I like it." It brought back a memory he hadn't thought about in years and it had nothing to do with travel, except that it had been part of the reason he'd become a gypsy.

"My mother had a big shopping bag like this that went everywhere with us when I was little." He replaced the pretty little bag, remembering his mother's larger, battered one. "We didn't have a car, so we walked everywhere or sometimes took the bus, and she carried groceries, bills to be paid, everything in this bag. Every couple of months the paper would finally give out and we'd buy another one for thirty-five cents from a department store dispenser.''

Diane rolled dough between the palms of her hands and stopped to look at him. She smiled hesitantly. ''Did you have a happy childhood, or a difficult one?''

He didn't even have to think twice. ''It was happy. I had everything I needed. My mother loved me and I was always aware of that. But I did miss having a father.''

''Did he pass away or leave?''

''Neither. He never existed.'' That always hurt a little to think about. He was an adult. He knew that to have any peace of mind one has to accept that your life is your life and you simply have to deal with how things are. But under it all was always the wish that, for a while at least, things could have been different. ''Well, of course he existed or I wouldn't. But he was never part of my life, apparently never cared that he had a son.''

Diane's eyes widened and softened. He mistook the look for pity for a moment, then realized it was just the empathy she felt for everyone.

"Do you know who he was?"

He nodded. "My mother was a bank teller, and he worked on a construction site across the street. Came in every Friday night to cash his check. They went out a couple of times, then the crew moved on to another job and she found herself pregnant with me. He never returned her calls."

"I'm sorry." She moved as though to touch his arm, then realizing her hands were covered in flour, artlessly rubbed her forearm against his upper arm in a gesture of sympathy. He felt it reach right inside him. She went back to forming balls out of cookie dough.

"It's all right," he said. "I think being limited to going to places we could walk to, or places that were on the bus line is what gave me wanderlust. The tight little circuit of my life as a child made me want broader horizons when I grew up. And that's served me well."

"Anna once told me that you leave for someplace different every year. That you work a local job to get enough money to take a trip. That's why you're working for her right now.''

He nodded. She pointed to a cup of cloves and he handed it to her.

''Right. And it's quite a plum job. Anna wants to make sure every detail is recorded for your parents because the kids are apparently so pleased they've found each other. So we negotiated a generous flat fee. That, along with my advance on the book will help me stay in Nouméa long enough to get every vital detail. I'll make enough money on the trip to support another trip, so my in-between jobs may no longer be necessary. The publisher says if they're pleased with these photographs, I could be invited to do a whole series they're planning on tropical islands. It's every photographer's dream career.''

''I'm happy for you,'' she said brightly. He wondered if he imagined a small and very subtle discordant sound in her voice.

She lined up the balls of dough on a cookie sheet and inserted a clove in the middle of each one. She reached again for the oven and he opened the door for her.

''Can you take a break from this to go out

for lunch?'' he asked. ''Or shall we order out for something?''

''Don't you have other things to do?'' She reached for the bowl of dough and formed another squadron of balls. Her momentum was remarkable.

''No.'' He reached for the phone book on a table at the edge of the kitchen. ''What are you in the mood for? Chinese? Pizza? Ribs?''

''Working with sweet stuff always makes me long for something hot and spicy.''

''Really.'' He leaned against the counter beside her. ''I wonder if working with sweet stuff would do the same for me.''

She turned to him laughing, thinking that he was offering to help, and ready to get him an apron. Then she saw the turbulent look in his eyes and realized the ''sweet stuff'' he talked about wasn't cookie dough. It was…her.

Completely distracted by being considered sweet stuff, she lost track of the hundreds of cookies yet unprepared, and forgot everything but the strong hand on her shoulder turning her to him, and the tender mouth opening over hers.

"Diane," he said in a whisper, the sound full of strong feeling.

Their lips had just made contact when the front door burst open. Diane and Jason drew apart in surprise.

Whitney hurried in, sobbing, her bulk making her awkward. She disappeared into a bedroom.

Tom and Claire stood in the open doorway, looking defeated.

"What happened?" Diane came to the edge of the dining room, floury hands held away from her.

Claire burst into tears. Tom put an arm around her shoulders and said grimly, "I think Whitney's changed her mind about giving up the babies."

CHAPTER FOUR

DIANE COULDN'T HELP the plaintive thought. "Oh, God." She tore off her apron, wiped her hands on it, and went to draw her troubled brother and Claire inside.

She settled them on the sofa, then directed quietly, "Tell me what she said."

Claire dabbed at her nose with a tissue. "She seemed a little tense this morning," Tom said, "but she was joking with us on the way to my partner's office. Then, in the middle of his explanation about how she could pick the college of her choice—" he stopped to expel a breath "—she just ran from the room in tears. Claire followed her to the ladies' room and they talked for a long time."

Claire nodded, tears still streaming down her face. "The worst part of all this," she said, gesturing with the crumpled tissue, "is that I understand her maternal feelings.

When I had to put up Jordan for adoption, I suffered all the agonies of separation and guilt, so I know what she's going through."

Tom wrapped an arm around her and rubbed her shoulder.

"But as I struggled through the next few months," Claire continued, gaining some control, "I realized I'd have never made it with a baby. I think giving us her babies would be the right thing for her." She leaned into Tom and said, on the brink of losing her composure again, "We'd love them so much." Then she drew a ragged breath and sat up a little straighter. "We don't want to pressure her, of course, so tell her she's welcome to call us any time if she wants to talk about it."

Diane, sitting on the other side of Tom, patted his shoulder. "I'm sorry. Thanks for being so understanding. I know what this means to both of you. I'll try to talk to her. Do you want some coffee? A drink?"

Claire shook her head. "We should probably go."

Diane walked them to the door. Claire stopped to give her a hug. "This is all really complicating your life, too, isn't it?"

Diane shrugged it off. "Life always feels complicated. And I suppose the more people you get into the equation, the worse it gets."

Tom leaned down to kiss Diane's cheek. "I'll be back to collect my cookies."

"Any time," she said.

Diane rested against the door for a moment after she closed it behind Tom and Claire. She'd suspected this morning that Whitney's concerns were more than a passing thought.

"Anything I can do?" Jason asked. He stood in the middle of the living room, shrugging into his jacket.

She looked into his concerned expression and longed for the kiss that had never quite happened. "Unless you have a degree in child psychology, I don't think so."

"Sorry. Then, much as I hate to, I should leave you and Whitney alone. I put my card with my phone and cell numbers on that bulletin board in your kitchen. If you need me, call. Otherwise, I'll see you tomorrow afternoon to decorate the hotel banquet room."

She walked him to the door. "I enjoyed hearing about your travels," she said, holding the door open for him. "Felt a little as though I finally got to take a trip."

"I enjoyed watching you bake." He put a hand to her cheek and rubbed a thumb over her cheekbone. Her body reacted as though she'd been intimately touched. "But we have to spend some time together that doesn't involve my camera and your rolling pin."

It was on the tip of her tongue to say, *but you're going away in a few weeks, and I may never get to leave Austin, the way things are looking.* But she suddenly didn't care about what was going to happen in two weeks or for the rest of her life.

Now seemed critically important. "I'd like that—if we can find the time. There are family events for you to photograph every day until Christmas."

"If I know you're willing," he said. "I'll find a way."

She looked into his eyes. "I'm willing."

He leaned down to kiss her gently. "Then, I'm invincible. I'll let you know the plan."

"Okay."

The elevator dinged to announce the

doors opening on the fourth floor. He loped to catch them before they closed again, then leaned out the elevator to blow her a kiss.

She waved, then stepped back into the apartment, everything inside her fluttering with this new discovery. She *was* a sexual being.

She went to Whitney's room and found her pacing the floor, rubbing her swollen stomach and sobbing.

Diane drew her down onto the edge of the bed. "Whitney, try to calm down," she advised gently. "This isn't good for you or the twins. Can you tell me what happened?"

"Do they hate me?" Whitney asked between gulps for air. "I know they have to hate me!" She didn't have to explain who she was talking about.

"No, they don't," Diane assured her, rubbing between her shoulder blades. "Claire experienced this herself, remember? She understands what you're going through."

"I thought I could do it," Whitney wept. "I really did. I thought I could just be big and strong and know what was best for my babies and do it! Then the lawyer was explaining that they were going to pay for my college and for me to stay in the dorms and give me spending money so I wouldn't have to have a job and study, too, and—'' she raised both hands helplessly ''—I felt like I was selling my babies so that I could have an easy life!''

''Whitney.'' Diane held her as she collapsed into fresh sobs. ''First of all, life is never easy. You would be very fortunate to have someone paying for your education, but how you use it and what you choose to make of yourself with it is entirely up to you and how hard you're willing to work. Tom and Claire aren't trying to buy your babies from you, they're just so grateful that you wanted them to raise them, that they were trying to do whatever they could to help you.''

''I know,'' Whitney said tearfully. ''I didn't mean they were trying to buy them, I just meant that I felt like I was selling them! And I feel them move and I hear their heartbeats when we go to the doctor's and...I don't know what to do! I feel like they're *mine* and I'll hate myself every single day if I don't keep them.''

Diane tried to remain calm to keep Whitney calm.

"Sweetie, I'm not trying to tell you what to do, and usually the best way to decide what to do is by whether or not it feels right—not if it feels *good,* but if it feels *right.* But in this case, your maternal instincts are all entangled in the situation, so you have to think about not what feels right to Whitney, but what feels right to the mother of your twins."

"I know." Whitney turned to her eagerly. "I think it'd be great if I could go to college and keep the twins. I know Tom and Claire wouldn't be paying for it for me then, but I have good grades, and I have one more year of high school to go. Maybe I can get a scholarship." She dabbed at her eyes, then sat up and swallowed. "Maybe my aunt will let me stay with her with the twins until then, maybe I can get a scholarship and a job, and…maybe I'd do all right."

A hundred pitfalls to that theory lined up in Diane's mind but she couldn't give them voice at the moment and destroy Whitney's fragile hope. She tried to imagine herself at that age even thinking she could do what Whitney proposed, and couldn't summon up the picture. Their father had always been a moral force in their lives, though very busy. But Tom had always kept an eye on her boyfriends, Suzanne had always kept an eye on her, and there'd been enough love in her home that she hadn't had to try to find it in the arms of a football player. She knew just how fortunate she'd been.

But she did feel that she had to come down on the side of Whitney's aunt. "Bear in mind that you're asking a lot of your aunt. She's over sixty. It's hard to have one baby around when you're older, much less two."

"But I'd do everything! I would!"

"It's certainly something to think about," Diane said reasonably. "And it's not as though you're having the twins tomorrow. You have a little time to decide what to do."

"Aunt Joyce is at my cousin's for a couple of days, but she's supposed to be back to sign the closing papers on the house on the twenty-third. We're supposed to get together and talk about my moving in. I'll ask her how she'd feel about it."

Whitney prayed that Aunt Joyce had a generous heart.

The doorbell rang and Diane left Whitney to wash her face while she answered it. It was a delivery boy from a nearby Chinese restaurant with Mongolian beef and Kung Pao chicken.

"Oh!" Diane exclaimed and went to look for her purse, thinking Jason had placed their order for lunch before realizing that he would have to leave.

"It's paid for, ma'am!" the boy called after her, holding the bag out to her. "Mr. Morris orders from us all the time, except that we usually deliver it to his darkroom. He charged it to his account and told me to tell you to enjoy it."

Diane took the bag and thanked the boy, still digging in her purse for a tip.

"He charged the tip, too," he said. "Have a good day, ma'am."

Diane carried the bag into the kitchen, the spicy aroma of Szechuan cuisine mingling pleasantly with the ingredients in the cookies. This was like a metaphor for her life, she thought, opening the bag with anticipation. The scent of cookies was her life so far. The introduction of the spice that made every sense come alive with anticipation was Jason's arrival into that life.

CHAPTER FIVE

BY THE MIDDLE of the following afternoon, Diane had twelve hundred cookies, plus or minus a few, stored in tins and under foil, covering every surface in the kitchen and several in other parts of the house. She delivered Tom's promised half dozen to his office. He greeted her with determined good cheer and poured her a cup of coffee.

"I'm working on Whitney," she promised him, sipping at the strong brew. "I'm sure given time to think things through, she'll come to the right decision. This is interesting stuff," she added, indicating her cup. "Whose idea was it to add charcoal?"

He scolded her with an arched eyebrow. "Coffee should have substance."

"Yes, but not texture." She took another sip and pretended to chew. "Does this come with dental floss?"

He shook his head at her, his expression

mournful. "Could you please be nice to me? My life's a little chaotic at the moment."

"How's Claire?"

"Stoic but miserable."

"This isn't going to come between you, is it?" she asked gently. "I know how desperately she wants a family."

He shook his head. "No. We're pretty solid. But I hate to see her unhappy. And I was kind of looking forward to the prospect of a baby in each arm. But we understand Whitney's dilemma. That's part of what makes it so difficult. It'd be easier if we could rant and rave, but love's more complicated than that. Speaking of which..." He seemed to come out of his own problems with a sigh to focus on her. "Jason Morris certainly seems to consider you his favorite subject."

"I like him, too," she admitted. Tom had always been a good confidant, even if his accomplishments made her feel inadequate. "But he's leaving in a couple of weeks and I'm...not."

"You could."

"How?"

"Whitney'll be moving in with her aunt

soon. You can buy yourself out of your contract at school.''

"To what purpose?"

"I heard him ask you to meet him in Nouméa. You're always planning trips that end up taking a back seat to your responsibilities. Maybe it's time to put yourself first. I like him. Suzanne likes him. She had him take a family portrait of Doug and her and the triplets.''

Diane put her half-empty coffee cup aside. "I didn't know that.''

"She said he was really good with the triplets. Managed to get each of their little personalities to emerge.'' He leaned slightly forward, forearms on his desk, and looked into her face. "He even seems to be doing something for yours. You look like someone's lit a candle inside you. Are you in love, sis?''

She stood abruptly. "This coffee's obviously corroding your brain,'' she said, turning to frown into his grinning face as he walked her to the door. "We've been on each other's nerves since the day I met him, and while we're learning to coexist, we're still too different for anything to ever come of this. And love is definitely not in the picture.''

He reached around her to open his office door. "You must be looking at a different picture.''

She stepped into the outer office, determined to change the subject. "Are you coming to help me hang maps for the reception?''

"We'll be there. What time?''

"I'll call you.''

Tom caught her arm as she would have walked away and wrapped her in a hug. "Thanks for the cookies,'' he said.

She hugged back. "You're welcome. I'd say thanks for the coffee, but it's already dissolved my molars.''

He gave her a playful shove toward the elevators. "Be gone, devil child,'' he laughed.

Diane was shocked to find Jason sitting in the lobby of Tom's office building. He held a dozen red roses wrapped in glittering cellophane in one arm, and a box of what appeared to be chocolates in the other. She stared at him in astonishment when he stood and came to her.

"What are you doing here?" she demanded.

"Courting you," he replied seriously.

"How did you know I was here?"

"Whitney told me."

"But—" she indicated the flowers and candy "—I don't understand."

"This is how courtships are conducted," he said, as though surprised she didn't know. "Haven't you *ever* been courted?"

"Once by a boy in college," she replied as he handed her the flowers, then took her arm and led her toward the double glass doors. "He gave me a subscription to *Atlantic Monthly*."

"Ah. An intellectual. They don't make the best romantics, you know."

"It didn't last very long."

"The relationship or the subscription?"

"Neither. His check bounced, and we had a falling out over politics. I'm a screaming liberal. He wasn't."

Jason nodded sympathetically. "Just put all that behind you. Artists know how to do this." In the parking lot, he led her to a freshly washed, but obviously hard-used, gray Jeep. It had none of the refinements of the Grand Cherokee. This was the basic Jeep—an old workhorse. He opened the door on the passenger side.

"But my car..." She held the roses like a baby and pointed in the direction of her little red import.

"We'll come back for it," he said and walked around to the driver's side.

"Where are we going?" she asked.

"On a picnic."

"In December?"

"Trust me."

She was willing to. She'd been thrilled to see him so unexpectedly, and her delight in his presence was growing by the moment. He was smiling and relaxed, and she was beginning to feel that way, too.

"Well, if you know so much about romance," she teased, "how come the candy box isn't heart-shaped?"

He cast her a grinning glance as he started the Jeep. "Because the oblong box holds more. Ready?"

She nodded. Oh, she was ready.

He drove to Cahill's Austin Palace, left the Jeep in the care of a parking attendant, and led her inside. The lobby was lavishly decorated with gold garland hung with crystal ornaments and an eighteen-foot tree trimmed with pearl strings and more crystal.

She presumed their destination was the dining room, and was surprised and a little off balance when he took her to the elevators instead.

"Where are we going?" she asked worriedly.

"To one of the penthouse suites," he replied, holding the door open for her onto an empty car.

She felt a rush of bitter disappointment. Feeling her mood change from sparkling warmth to dead-of-winter frost, she folded her arms and remained stubbornly on the carpeting. "If presumption is your idea of romance," she said, her voice reflecting her mood's change of temperature, "then you're not the artist you thought you were."

She turned to walk away and found her direction reversed when he caught her arm and pulled her onto the elevator.

"You're the one who's being presumptuous," he returned, catching her wrists as she struggled with him. The elevator doors closed and the car began its ascent. "I told you I was taking you on a picnic."

"In a hotel suite?"

"The suite is famous for its balcony overlooking the rooftops of downtown." He loosened his grip on her and she yanked away from him to back into the opposite corner. "The day's threatening rain off and on. I thought we could picnic on the balcony, and move indoors if it does rain. I swear that getting you in bed never crossed my mind. I just wanted you to see Austin the way the birds and angels see it."

She studied him suspiciously.

He relented with the smallest smile. "Okay, it did cross my mind, but I dismissed it. You said you love hilltop views of old cities, and this was the best I could do without an airplane ticket."

The doors parted on the penthouse floor and he stepped out into the hallway, holding the door for her again.

She studied him from her corner, when she heard the sound of a lively trumpet, and the mellow harmony of male voices. "What's that?" she asked.

"Mariachis," he replied. "On foreign

picnics, you might hire gypsies. In Texas, you invite mariachis.''

Three men in brightly beaded sombreros and patterned pants and shirts appeared at the elevator doors, guitars strumming, voices raised in a lilting love song.

Diane's frosty mood melted completely.

JASON OFFERED her his hand. Her indecision of a moment ago disappeared as she took it. She looked into his eyes and he saw the trust return—and was confused when that both pleased and worried him. Trust was a good thing. Why should that upset him?

He put that thought aside and concentrated on proving himself the romance artist he'd claimed to be. The blanket he'd set up earlier was spread across the balcony, complete with several cushions, and globe candles were placed on a small table.

As promised, the dining room had delivered a basket filled with beautifully prepared picnic foods, and a waiter Jason had generously tipped earlier stood waiting for them, wine bottle ready to pour. Behind him, San Antonio spread out like a glimpse of old

Mexico, magically blended with the drama of big-city high-rises.

"Jason!" Diane breathed. "How did you arrange all this?"

"I'm a photographer," he replied, offering her a hand as she folded into a sitting position on the blanket. "I'm used to bringing props together on a moment's notice." He arranged a pillow beside her. "Lean an elbow on that and we'll start with some gulf shrimp."

The sky was bright at the moment, the temperature in the low sixties. She wore jeans with a shirt and jacket, but he tossed a hotel blanket over her knees to be sure she was warm enough.

"This is rather elegant for picnic fare," she said, biting into a shrimp.

He gestured toward the fancy spread. "This is a picnic the way an artist—a romantic artist—would arrange it."

As the mariachis played, Diane and Jason went from shrimp to Waldorf salad, to roasted capons and vegetables. The waiter refilled their wineglasses several times, then offered them strawberry tarts with cream for dessert.

"I can't do it!" Diane pleaded, pushing the plate away. "Thank you, but I don't have room for a sip of water!"

"Would you pack the rest to go, please?" Jason asked the waiter. When he left, Jason propped the cushions against the half-closed French doors and he and Diane sat side by side, looking out on the city. The Mariachis continued to play quietly just inside the room.

"My goal," Diane said, "will be to do this in every major capital of the world. Find the right balcony on the right hotel and eat the best food while feeding my soul on the view of the city."

"A worthy ambition," he agreed lazily. "But I don't think it's an activity for one." He put an arm around her and drew her closer until she could lean against his shoulder. "*This* is the perfect way to do those things, all wrapped up with someone you..." He hesitated, something seeming to block his next word. He tried to think around it, but kept meeting the same obstacle. "Someone important," he finally said.

"I didn't want you to be important to me." She leaned her weight comfortably against him. "But I didn't seem to have much to say about it. The timing's bad and the situation's hopeless, yet—" she tipped her head back to look into his face "—you're all I think about."

That admission went right to his head, then settled in the region of his heart, repeating itself to him—you're all she thinks about. You're all she thinks about.

He turned her so that she lay in his arms, then he lowered his mouth to take hers. She reached up for him eagerly. They kissed with all the passion of two people finally realizing what it means to find a soul mate. He felt as though he reached inside her, sounding the depths of her feelings for him. And she snared the very air he breathed, this contact deeper and more urgent than anything he'd ever experienced.

"Can I change my mind about the bed?" he whispered as he traced kisses along her jaw.

She groaned softly. "This was so...so perfect." Her arms were wrapped around his neck, her lips avid as they kissed his eyelids, his cheekbones, the rim of his ear.

For the first time that he could remember

in his adult life, he felt his insides tremble. It was also the first time he remembered wanting a woman the way he wanted her. Lust and longing had combined into a formidable force and didn't seem to care that he'd seen her for the first time only two weeks before, and had actually established a relationship with her only three days ago.

"Make love with me," he said, his lips wandering down her throat into the V of her shirt collar.

She nipped his ear as he kissed her collarbone, then she framed his face in her hands and pulled him away from her, leaning her forehead against his as she drew a deep breath.

"No," she said softly. "This is just the kind of thing that gets kids into trouble."

"But we're not kids."

She kissed his cheek. "But trouble is still trouble, and I have a lot to contend with right now. I want to be absolutely sure of what I feel before I make love with you. This has happened so fast."

He grinned. "When you're used to dealing in shutter speeds, it's not that fast at all." But he was grateful for any glimmer of hope. "Just tell me that our making love is on your mind, too."

She used her hands on his shoulder to lever herself to her feet. "It's in every cell in my body," she said, then offered him a hand up. "It wouldn't make any sense because you can't stay and I can't go, so I don't know why I'm even thinking about it."

"Maybe," he said, accepting her hand and springing lightly to his feet, "I'm finally affecting you the same way you affect me. I'm growing into you, too. I'm becoming part of you."

She wrapped her arms around him and held tightly. "This can't work, can it?"

There was desperation in her voice, in the way she held him. He held her tightly in return to reassure her. "It's working now, isn't it?"

She drew back to look him frankly in the eye. "It's feeling wonderful," she said. "But is that the same as working?"

He couldn't imagine why she had to borrow trouble. "It's Christmas, Diane. Everything works at Christmas."

They held each other for a long moment, then she drew away to smile happily into his face. "This was a wonderful and most romantic afternoon. You're every bit the artist you claim to be."

"What are your plans for the rest of the afternoon?"

"I ordered greens from the florist to decorate the front of our favor bags. Suzanne and a couple of Megan's daughters are coming to help me make them."

He patted his pants pockets for keys. "I'll drive you there, then we'll pick up your car."

"You're coming home with me?" She looked both pleased and alarmed at that possibility.

He put an arm around her shoulders and drew her inside. "I have to photograph the event, remember?"

In the cool suite, untouched by the lavish picnic on the balcony, the bedroom door beyond stood open invitingly.

"You're sure you don't want to make love with me?" he teased, pointing toward the inviting bed, hung with sheer draperies.

SHE COULD IMAGINE being with him in that bed, body to body, mouths touching, hands exploring.

She caught his arm and pulled him toward the front door before her feet could move in the direction of the bedroom. ''Sorry. We have a date with holly and pine.''

''Okay—but I'll be pine-ing for you,'' he said, slanting her a glance to see if she'd caught the pun.

She rolled her eyes at him in the hallway. ''That was hopelessly corny,'' she scolded with a laugh.

''Corny stuff,'' he retorted, ''is an artist's stock in trade.''

She caught his arm and pulled him toward the front door before her feet could move in the direction of the boudoir. "Sorry. We have a date with—"

"Okay—not interrupting me; you'll be sorry. Suddenly this is cute," he said.

CHAPTER SIX

THERE WERE CHILDREN and babies all over Diane's apartment. Whitney, the self-appointed sitter and leader of games, kept the toddlers occupied in the living room, while the babies slept in carriers on the floor.

Greens were spread on newspaper in the middle of the kitchen table, and four women sat around it performing various tasks. Suzanne punched two holes close together on the front of each bag, Dana Maitland, one of Megan's daughters-in-law, strung a length of foil ribbon through so that both ends dangled, Ellie Cassidy helped Diane attach greens to the front of the bags, and Suzanne put the finishing touch by curlings the ends of the ribbon. The room was aromatic and the mood festive.

By nine o'clock that night, two hundred bags had been finished and stacked in boxes and baskets.

Jason photographed every step of the operation from several angles, then took pictures of the sleeping babies. He wandered into the living room where Whitney now read a storybook to the children gathered around her on the sofa.

The women heard giggles and laughter from the living room.

"He's gorgeous," Dana remarked.

"Diane's seeing him," Suzanne contributed with a so-there look at her sister. "He thinks she's very photogenic. He wants her to go with him to—"

"Suze!" Diane stopped her with a sharp command that she turned quickly to a smile of apology. "I'm sorry," she said to the little group that were about to become her stepsisters. "I didn't mean to shout, but she's one of those big sisters who thinks it's her job to point up my achievements to everyone." Then realizing how that sounded, she backpedaled. "Not that seeing Jason is an achievement. I just—"

Ellie patted her hand. "You don't have to explain to us how sisters interact. And Anna is always doing the same thing to all of us."

"Yes," Dana agreed. "And snagging him

would be an achievement. He's obviously brilliant, and Anna says he has a book contract to photograph some island—"

"Nouméa," Diane clarified.

"That's right. You're the social studies expert."

"Hardly an expert," Diane corrected quickly. "I'm just fascinated by people and places."

"Is Nouméa where he wants you to go with him?" Ellie asked.

Dana chided her for asking, but she insisted. "Come on. We're all going to be sisters in a couple of days. We have a right to weigh in on what's going on. Don't we?"

Diane blinked, flattered by her concern, but a little worried about acquiring more sisters like Suzanne.

"You may weigh in," Diane said with a smile, "as long as you don't expect me to follow your advice."

"Fair enough," Ellie said, leaning closer. "So, are you going?"

"And, did he propose yet?" Dana prodded teasingly. "You've known him just a few weeks!"

Diane's answer did not seem required

when the sisters got into a discussion on the merits of marriage and the number of relationships that progressed rapidly because of instant attraction. It soon became a rhapsodic recounting of the pleasures and satisfactions of their daily lives. Suzanne had a lot to contribute in anticipation of her own marriage to Doug McKay after a courtship of less than a month.

Diane stood to make a fresh pot of coffee and saw Jason sitting cross-legged on the floor in front of Whitney and the toddlers leaning close on each side of her. Jason focused on one enraptured little face after the other. Then Diane watched him lower the camera and simply stare at the little tableau with a thoughtful smile.

Something inside her melted into a warm puddle.

The group started to disperse at ten. Thanking everyone for their help and assuring them that she could finish on her own, Diane distributed jackets and helped put coats on toddlers.

She was sending off her guests when she realized Suzanne stood in the middle of the living room with Fran and Kimmie, two of the triplets. Jason was helping himself to a cup of coffee.

"Where's Edie?" Diane asked about the third one.

"Whitney took her into the bathroom to wash her face," Suzanne replied, glancing at her watch. "She really got into her cocoa. But they've been a few minutes. Would you—"

Suzanne's request went unfinished when the sound of a child in tears came from the direction of the bathroom. Diane and Suzanne hurried down the hall, but were intercepted by Whitney coming up with the tearful Edie on her hip. Whitney was sobbing.

"What happened?" Diane asked as Suzanne scooped up the child.

"Nothing," Whitney said, sniffling and patting Edie's back. "I'm sorry I upset her, Suzanne. I was just…thinking, and I started crying, and I guess I just frightened her."

"And you were all having such a good time tonight." Suzanne hugged the little girl to her. "Everything's okay. Whitney just has a tummy ache. She didn't mean for you to get scared."

A tummy ache indeed. Diane suspected

that what had upset Whitney did have to do with the little residents in her tummy.

"I'm sorry, Edie," Whitney said, ruffling her hair.

"Why don't you give her a smile?" Suzanne cajoled.

Edie leaned heavily on Suzanne's shoulder, clearly tired and in no mood to pacify the adults.

"I'll help you out to the car," Diane volunteered. "That's a lot of little bodies to keep track of with one of them in your arms." Whitney had gone back down the hall toward the bathroom. Jason had a large plastic bag and was sweeping bent and broken greens into it with his hand. "I'll be right back," she promised.

He waved her off. "I'll put on the kettle."

In the elevator, Suzanne frowned at Diane, who had Fran and Kimmie by the hands. "I heard Whitney changed her mind about letting Tom and Claire take her babies."

"She's upset and confused," Diane defended. "She doesn't know what she wants."

Suzanne blew air theatrically. "I love

these girls, but I can tell you I'm grateful I wasn't around when they were all in diapers, or just learning to walk. Multiples are fun, but they really do multiply the work. And I can't imagine being ready for what it takes at sixteen.''

''But you and Doug are okay?''

Suzanne blushed. Diane couldn't believe her eyes. For someone who'd been so sure she didn't want the responsibility of a family, she had done a rather remarkable about-face.

''We're more than okay. We're...we're stupendous!''

''Wow.''

''Yeah.'' Suzanne's grin went from ear to ear. ''You wouldn't believe how good it can be when it's good.''

She could certainly imagine, Diane thought. She helped secure the triplets into their car seats, then gave Suzanne a grateful hug. ''Thanks for coming to help. Especially with all your new duties.'' She indicated the triplets.

''I was happy to. After the holidays, it'll be back to routines for all of us. The girls will be in daycare while I'm at work, so I'm doing my best to bond and build our relationship now. See you day after tomorrow to put up all the maps.''

"If you're too busy, I can manage.''

"No. This wedding is special. I want to do my part. I love seeing Daddy so happy. And then Tom and Claire are like a pair of children— Well, they were until Whitney…'' she added regretfully. "It breaks my heart, you know. I mean, I understand Whitney's confusion, of course, but after Claire's little boy… It's just so sad all around.''

Diane hugged her again. "Well, I think you're all giving up too soon. I'm trusting that Whitney's good sense will kick in.''

Suzanne shook her head wryly. "You're always such an optimist, but let's hope so. Thanks for coming down with me.''

"Sure.'' The triplets nodded sleepily in their seats. Holiday dinners were going to be so much more interesting now, Diane thought as she waved Suzanne off and hurried back upstairs.

JASON FOUND A handheld vacuum in the utility closet in the kitchen and crawled with it under the kitchen table to be thorough. The pale linoleum looked like a forest floor, thick with pine needles and red berries. He cleaned the seats of the chairs, then folded up the newspapers spread on the table and carried it to the garbage bag left out for the mess.

When he returned to the living room, he found Whitney standing there, her face blotchy and swollen, a crumpled tissue in her hand. "I was coming out to do that," she said, her voice raspy. She looked miserable.

Jason's heart went out to her. "Just finished," he said, pulling a chair out for her. "And I put the kettle on. Want some... What will you have? Tea? Cocoa?"

The kettle whistled and she went past him to take it off the burner. "I'll make it. We have an orange spice tea that's pretty good."

He replaced the place mats Diane had removed to create a worktable. "When I was a kid my mother used to make Russian Tea using an orange-flavored breakfast drink, instant tea and some other stuff. I always liked that."

Whitney took down three cups and a box of tea. "When my mother was in a good mood, she'd make a pot of Chinese tea and we'd share it and talk about all the things she was going to do when she had some money.''

Jason put a pot of Christmas greens in the middle of the table. ''My mom and I had a lot of those conversations, too. She was single, though, and worked a lot, and there was never enough left over for the big dreams.''

Whitney nodded. ''Us neither, only my mom doesn't work a lot. She's always looking for the guy who's going to support her in the way she dreams of living. But all she seems to find are men like her who are waiting for someone else to do it for them.''

Jason studied Whitney's face, its youthful lines still curved and full, and thought how sad it was that so many unloved and neglected children sought relief from their loneliness and wanting by giving birth to babies who would probably end up victims of the same situation.

He, at least, had had a mother who was clearly in charge, who always saw to it that he had everything he needed, and who knew and understood her responsibilities. He'd never questioned his value as a human being, or felt required to validate his existence by creating another life.

"I'm sorry you've had such a tough time," he said, at a loss as to how to comfort her. She faced such an enormous decision. And the pain it caused her was because she cared.

She carried cups to the table, her quick glance at him showing surprise at his offer of sympathy. She sat on one side of the table, and he took the other.

"My dad left when I was four," she said. "Was your mom divorced?"

He remembered having this conversation with Diane. "No. My mom wasn't married."

"Like me," she said after a moment.

"Yeah," he replied.

"But she was a good mother."

"A wonderful mother."

"So…" She sipped her tea, then asked cautiously, hopefully, "So it was okay that you didn't have a dad?"

He had to be honest. "No," he said. "It was never okay. I had a home and enough to eat, and I did well in school, and my mom and I got along really well and we were happy.''

Whitney watched him, her eyes wide and anguished, waiting for him to go on. ''But every single day of my life, I was aware that I didn't have a father, and I couldn't help thinking that everything would have felt a little more right if I'd had one. When I was little and I was scared, Mom was a lot of comfort. But when I was older, and the fears got scarier, I really wished there was a man between us and all the things that could hurt us. And I'd have liked a guy to talk to about girls and sex and a million other important things.''

It was only when Whitney made a sound of distress and he reached across the table to cover her hand, that he saw Diane standing in the doorway. He hadn't realized she'd returned.

''I don't know what to do!'' Whitney wept.

Diane went to Whitney's chair and wrapped her arms around her. ''It's a tough decision,'' she said gently. ''Of course it's confusing.''

''I sat Edie on the sink in the bathroom,''

Whitney said, her voice tight and high, "and I was washing her face and then it hit me. If I give my babies up, I'll never see what they look like at four years old. I mean, if Claire and Tom took them, I'd *see* them, but they wouldn't be mine. But if I kept them…" She looked into Jason's face and the pain he saw in her eyes made him feel like a monster. "Would they always be wondering why they didn't have a dad? Or where he was? Even if I made it through college and got a good job, I wouldn't be able to fix that. Oh!" Whitney straightened with a suddenness that surprised Diane. She sat still a moment, both hands to her stomach, then relaxed and said with a quick, nervous laugh. "Just a kick. But they must have been working together. It was pretty hard."

"It's late," Diane said, urging her out of her chair, "and it's been a long day. Why don't you go to bed?"

"Okay." Whitney had wept away her makeup and looked tired and suddenly more mature. She frowned across the table at Jason. "Do you still miss having a father?"

He nodded. "I'm finally past needing protection or advice, but I'll always feel…fatherless." He was surprised by how difficult that was to tell her. He knew it hurt her to know that a woman in her same position had done the absolute best she could, and on some level, it couldn't be enough.

"Good night," she said, then turning to hug Diane, went off to bed.

When the bedroom door closed behind Whitney, Diane came around the table toward Jason. Her step was determined, her eyes riveted on him. She thought he'd done the wrong thing. He'd wondered if it was fair to tell Whitney the gritty truth when she was in such an emotional turmoil, but he'd thought truth was always the right choice. The camera always found it.

He braced himself to withstand her maternal anger. But when she sat in his lap and looped both arms around his neck, he was confused. And that confusion thickened when she kissed him, deeply and thoroughly.

"That's for kindly but honestly making a better case for giving up her babies than I ever could," she said. Then she kissed him again with the same intensity, but with a tenderness wrapped in it that was more comfort than reward.

"And that," she said as she drew back and kissed his forehead, "is because I'm sorry you missed so much in not having a father."

"You didn't have a mother," he pointed out, unwilling to accept praise, but unwilling to do anything that would make her move. "And you seem to be a complete human being."

"But I was twelve when she died, and I had the memory of her love. You didn't have that kind of backup."

"My mother did her best to be everything to me—it just isn't possible."

"I know." She held him close and rested her head atop his.

He wondered if there was a more desirable place in the world than pressed against her bosom. He didn't think so.

"You cleaned up for me," she said after a moment. "Thank you."

"Sure."

"You have to go home." She got to her feet suddenly. He followed her, raising an eyebrow at her sudden change of mood.

"This means you're still not sure how you feel about me?" he asked.

She looked into his eyes, a surprising frankness in her smile. "No, it means I'm sure I'm in love with you. But this isn't the time or place."

"Then name it," he said, reaching for her, "and I'll be there."

"It'll present itself," she said. "We have to be patient."

"You may have to be patient." He grabbed his camera and his jacket, and let her lead him toward the door. "But I'm going to make a fuss until it does."

She giggled and kissed him and pushed him out the door.

CHAPTER SEVEN

EVERY MEMBER OF the Maitland and the
Blake families showed up to help decorate
for the reception and brought maps. There
were road maps, old, outdated maps, pro-
motional maps of Texas distributed years
ago by a bank, maps from travel brochures.

"The plan," Diane said to the assembled
group as they all looked around worriedly at
the large room, "is to make a sort of border
of the maps at about eye level. Austin had
one of his painters come in and score off a
border for us—that's those two blue pencil
lines you see. Just place your maps straight
between the lines or at an arty angle—whatever you prefer—and we'll tack them up
with this sticky stuff." She held up a wad
of the tacky adhesive. "Then that same
painter is coming back when we're finished
to put a coat of clear sealer over it." She
smiled. "If we do a good job, he's going to

leave it up and rename this The Grand Tour Room. If we don't, it comes down right after the wedding.''

Amid nervous laughter and earnest conversations on how to place the maps correctly, everyone went to work.

Claire appeared at Diane's elbow with a colorful road map of West Texas. ''I noticed Whitney isn't here,'' she said worriedly. ''I hope it isn't because Tom and I are here.''

''Oh, no,'' Diane reassured her, holding her shopper's map of London to the wall with one hand while giving Claire her attention. ''Her aunt invited her to dinner and to spend the night. She moved into the new house today. I guess she wants to set some ground rules about their living together.''

Claire looked relieved. ''Good. I was hoping she wasn't reluctant to see us because of what's happened.'' She leaned a shoulder against the wall, fidgeting with the map she held. ''I'm sure we'll find another baby somewhere who needs a good home. I just related to Whitney's plight and I felt a sort of bond, you know?''

Diane put a hand to her shoulder. ''I know. And she might still...''

Claire shook her head. ''If Tom and I are hanging around as though ready to pounce on her when the babies come, she'll never be able to relax and have a safe birth. Tom and I talked about it and we were going to tell her tonight that she doesn't have to worry about us being upset and disappointed. I'm sure we'll find a baby.''

Diane gave her a quick hug. ''And that'll be the luckiest baby in the whole world. Come on. Help me with this map.''

It was midnight before they were finished, but the effect was surprisingly professional. Everyone stood back to look, turning in slow circles to admire the border that went around the entire room. There was a pleased silence.

Anna came to put an arm around Diane. ''I suggest you quit teaching and come to work for me full-time,'' she said, squeezing her close. ''You have great ideas—and even better than that, the cleverness to see them through! When Austin's man comes in tonight to glaze over the border, it's going to look as though the finest decorator and craftsmen got together to do it.''

''Yeah,'' R. J. Maitland said. He was the oldest brother and president of Maitland Ma-

ternity. "And actually it was just the combined efforts of the Maitlands and the
Blakes!"

There was laughter and a smattering of
applause.

Anna put one arm around his shoulders
and the other around Tom's as everyone
continued to stare. "We may be invincible
together."

Jason, Diane had noticed, had been all
over the place photographing the process.
He stood on a chair, then a table, then a
ladder for an aerial view. He shot hands at
work, faces turned toward each other in conversation, in laughter, in serious discussion.

Diane had little opportunity to speak with
him, but saw the unspoken message in his
eyes. "Tonight," it said. "Tonight is the
time. This is the place."

Everyone was preparing to leave when
Austin appeared with several waiters bearing
trays of champagne-filled glasses. "I think
the uniting of the Maitlands and the Blakes
deserves a toast," he said. "We know Megan and Hugh are solid, but it's a blessing
to know that their children like each other
and can come together as a family, as a force

for good and—'' he looked around him at their handiwork, obviously searching for the right word ''—and wallpapering,'' he finally said on a laugh.

Other laughter joined his and every glass was raised.

But before he could make the toast, Anna turned to Jason, who was ready to photograph the moment, and said, ''Would you put that camera down and pick up a glass. You've been a part of this so long, we've voted you one of us.''

Jason appeared stunned for an instant, then put the camera down and took the last glass from the tray offered him. Diane winked at him across the circle they'd made in the middle of the room.

''To romantic love that lasts forever,'' Austin said. ''And to familial love that endures everything.''

Everyone drank.

''Please don't throw the glasses!'' Austin pleaded. ''Just put them back on the trays as you leave. We'll see you all in the dining room tomorrow night for the rehearsal dinner.''

There were hugs and handshakes as

everyone went their separate ways. The painter appeared to apply the glazing coat of sealant on the wall.

"Are you getting triple time for working at midnight?" Diane teased him as she gathered up her coat and purse.

"Overtime," he replied, "and a free weekend for the wife and me in the bridal suite. With three children under five, I can't tell you how much appeal that has to me. I'd do this standing on my head if I had to."

Diane laughed and left him to it—and found Jason waiting for her in the doorway. She went into his arms without saying a word. This night was special. A coming together of powerful forces—strong families, strong feelings, great love.

"I booked the room where we picnicked," he said softly, brushing his lips lightly against her cheek. "Only this time I'd maybe like us to use the bed and not the balcony," he whispered.

She wrapped her arms around him and kissed his lips, feeling curiously light-headed yet heavy-limbed. "Yes. Me, too."

He wrapped both arms around her and held tightly. "That's what I wanted to hear,'' he whispered. He led her to the elevators.

The suite was just as she remembered, except that she'd been unwilling to walk into the bedroom the day they were here. Their lives were complicated and his plans for the immediate future weren't entirely compatible with hers. Saying yes to what she felt for him would have been foolhardy.

But today there was hope. Whitney was about to move in with her aunt, and while Diane couldn't leave for Nouméa with Jason the week after New Year's because of her teaching contract, she could meet him during spring break, then spend the summer there.

There were red roses in a crystal vase on the coffee table in the suite's living room, and a bottle of champagne chilling in a bucket of ice on the bar into the kitchen.

''More champagne?'' Jason asked as he put his camera down on the bar.

Diane dropped her jacket and purse on the sofa and went to put her arms around him. ''More you,'' she replied.

HUMBLED BY the sincerity of her answer, Jason swept her into his arms and carried her to the bedroom. He had a vague impression of a lot of white, of lace and eyelet, and half a dozen fat pillows, but the focal point of his attention—even before Diane—was the tremor in his gut. This was important. This was…everything.

He swept all the pillows over the side and put her in the middle of the bed. She looped her arms around his neck and held on so that he was forced to come down with her.

Their kisses were hot and eager, their hands all over each other, removing clothing, pushing off undies and briefs, helping each other with stockings and socks and shoes.

Free of encumbrance, they lay on the cool bedsheet, blankets pulled up, and simply held each other, bodies in full and blissful contact from shoulder to toe.

"I've dreamed of holding you like this since the first time I saw you," he said, his hand tracing her back, shaping her hip. "I can't believe we're finally here."

She rubbed a knee along his thigh. "I know. I thought you were going to be like all those trips I never got to take. And yet—here we are."

He laughed softly. "So, you're likening me to a tropical vacation?"

She kissed him soundly. "No. I always plan to go to significant places where I'll learn things, connect with history."

"That makes me sound dull and old."

She nipped his shoulder. "Where I know the experience will change me," she said significantly.

Those words made lace of his usual iron will.

He spent the next two hours proving to her that he was indispensable. He touched her with passion and tenderness, his hands and his kisses saying all the things for which he simply hadn't the words.

She replied in kind, lips and fingertips running over him with the delight of discovery, then again with knowledge and confidence.

The newness of their lovemaking indulged and satisfied, they came together again explosively, desire given reign. Diane wrested control of the encounter from him at one point, and he let her, enjoying her bold exploration of him and the confidence with which she loved him.

When she began to tenderly torment him
with kisses down the middle of his body, he
turned them so that she lay on her back with
him astride her.

He entered her with a swift, sure thrust.
Her body rose to welcome him, enclose him.
Pleasure consumed him, but at the core of it
he was aware of his raw emotions, of a need
for her that he would never be free of now
that they'd made love.

CHAPTER EIGHT

DIANE LAY IN Jason's arms, feeling as though she'd been disassembled, then reassembled into the woman she'd always wanted to be. It wasn't that Jason had changed her, but that loving him had changed her. Now she understood what love was all about. It was like traveling to a new place without having to leave home. It was the newness of discovery mingled with the comfort of familiarity. It was…everything.

"Let's get married before I leave," Jason said, strumming his fingers up her bare arm atop the coverlet. "It'll keep me from going insane until you can meet me in the spring if I know we belong to each other."

"Yes," she said. But she wasn't sure it would prevent her from going insane.

"I'll do such a brilliant job on this book that they'll give me that other project so that we'll have a regular income and you can

travel with me. Then we'll come home occasionally for a few months so you can be
with your family and teach seminars or
something.''

"But I already have a regular income,"
she reminded him. "Even if I do nothing. I
have a substantial trust fund, and did a little
investing of my own. Fortunately I got out
before tech stocks dropped." She tipped her
head back to look into his face. "You're not
going to make a fuss about that, are you? I
mean, you're not going to insist we live on
your money and save mine, or something?"

He considered a minute. "No. I'm sure
you're used to a level of comfort I can't provide—at least not yet. But I have to do my
thing, just as you have to do yours. And
when we're living on the road, conditions
are sometimes primitive and money can't
change that. Is that going to be all right with
you?"

"Well, of course." She squeezed his
chest punitively. "You don't think I'm a
whiner, do you?"

"Of course not. I just want you to know
what to expect."

It sounded like the perfect life. It was hard

to believe it could be hers. "Do we buy a Winnebago?"

He laughed. "No. We downsize our daily lives so we can live out of backpacks and keep on the move."

"What about those few months at home?"

"We could keep your apartment. Or we could just keep this suite with its view of the city. That'd probably eat up your trust fund in a hurry."

"You underestimate my father's expertise at setting it up. I did notice that there are condos going up, two blocks over. We should check those out for the ideal view." She was suddenly, overwhelming tired and snuggled into his shoulder. "We have to be up early in the morning," she said with a yawn. "It's Christmas Eve, the rehearsal, the dinner."

"We should keep this room another night. Everything happens downstairs. You can use this room as your base of operations."

"You're forgetting Whitney."

"There're two other bedrooms. When is she moving in with her aunt?"

"I'm not sure. I'll know more when she comes back tomorrow." She yawned again.

He put her arm under the blanket and pulled the covers over her shoulder. "Go to sleep. We can talk about it in the morning."

AS IT HAPPENED, there wasn't time. They overslept. Diane got a call from Whitney on her cell phone saying she was home, and the front desk called the room to tell Diane that Austin wanted her to make sure the map border in the room to be used for the reception was to her liking before he put the furniture back in.

And Anna called Jason, wanting him to meet her at Megan's home to photograph the rehearsal of the flowergirls. They'd decided the lively little girls needed extra training to prevent unexpected shenanigans on their trip down the aisle.

"I don't want to be parted from you for a few hours," Jason said earnestly as they kissed goodbye in the lobby. "How am I going to deal with it for months at a time until spring break? And then I'll only have you for a week."

Diane clung to him, concerned about the

same thing. "I don't know. Other people deal with separation. I guess we'll have to, too."

"I don't want to."

"Neither do I."

"Then we'll have to think of something." He walked away with a pause at the door to wave.

She blew him a kiss.

He smiled and disappeared.

Diane headed home, thinking that there was no solution that she could see. Each of them was tied to contracts that could be broken only if they didn't care what happened to their futures—separately or collectively.

WHITNEY WAS TIDYING the kitchen when Diane arrived home.

"How's your aunt?" Diane asked as she dropped her purse on the table and went to the coffeepot, pulling the basket out to insert a fresh filter. "It's going to take a lot of coffee to get me through today. I hope you're drinking enough tea to keep up with me."

Whitney cast her a quick smile as she continued to scrub the counter top. "Aunt Joyce is fine. She says hi."

"Good. How's the house?"

"It's…cute."

Diane had been a teacher of teenagers long enough to recognize the troubled note in a voice trying hard to hide it.

Whitney continued to scrub.

Diane forgot the coffeepot as a niggling sense of foreboding crept along her spine. "What happened?" she asked gently.

Whitney went to the faucet to rinse the sponge, then would have gone back to her task if Diane hadn't intercepted her. She saw panic in the girl's eyes overlaid by an overwhelming sadness.

"I can't stay with her," Whitney said, "if I keep the babies."

"Oh, Whitney." Diane put an arm around her shoulders. "I'm sorry. But you have to see it from her perspective. Raising twin babies is an enormous job for a young person. Imagine how it would be for a woman in her sixties."

"But I would raise them!"

"Okay, then who would support you?"

"I'd get a job."

"Then who would watch the babies while you work?"

Whitney thought, her expression crumpling. "If you can't afford to pay a babysitter or a daycare," Diane continued, "your aunt would end up looking after them. Or you could do it, but then she'd have to support you, too. And who'd watch them when you had to go for groceries, or to the dentist, or just for a walk because you need a break?"

Whitney's eyes reflected her misery. "If I give them up, I'll hate myself always!"

Diane felt her own heart sink. She could certainly understand the aunt's position, but she couldn't turn the girl out. Her mistake hadn't been made carelessly, but rather on a desperate search for the love she'd never gotten elsewhere.

"You can stay with me until they're born," Diane said, her voice reverberating in the quiet kitchen, reminding her that she was no longer the only one affected by her decisions. She hesitated a moment, wondering how Jason would react to this news. "Then we'll...see how it goes."

Whitney's face brightened fractionally. "You're sure?"

"Yes."

"But...how will Jason feel? I mean, you two are getting pretty serious."

Diane thought it safer to leave that issue until later. "I'll explain it to him."

Whitney studied her a moment longer, then a genuine smile lit her face. She threw her arms around Diane and wept. "Thank you," she said. "Thank you. I know I can be a mom. I know I can do it."

Diane patted her back. Yes, she thought. But will I ever be a wife now that I've made this promise?

She tried calling Jason several times on his cell phone, but guessed he'd turned it off to give his attention to his work. She would tell him tonight, after the rehearsal dinner.

She went into the bedroom to try on her bridesmaid's dress again. There'd been so much partying the past several weeks, she hoped it still fit.

JASON PHOTOGRAPHED the wedding rehearsal, feeling a swell of pride when Diane followed the long, long line of casually clad attendants to the altar. Soon, he thought greedily, she would be the bride and not the bridesmaid.

Whitney waited in the third seat, keeping an eye on Suzanne's fiancée's triplets. While the minister gave instructions to the bride and groom and their attendants, Jason shouldered his camera and went to sit in the seat behind Whitney, but the little girls remembered him from the night in Diane's apartment and literally dragged him into their pew.

The moment he sat, he had a little girl on each knee and one hanging from his neck.

"They like you," Whitney said.

He wrapped his arms around them, trying to prevent the wriggling little bodies from ending up in heaps under the pew.

"Good thing," he said, as a patent-leather clad little shoe somehow clipped his chin. "I'd hate to see what they do to people they *don't* like."

"You like children?"

"Of course," he replied, as a small pair of arms tried to strangle him. "It's hard not to."

"Then you're okay about the babies?"

she asked. When he waited a beat, hoping a little thought would clarify her meaning, she added, ''Well, I know you're in love with Diane, and she's in love with you. You'll be okay with the twins living with you?''

He still didn't have a grasp on the conversation, though the part of it he did understand was starting to alarm him.

''Diane's keeping the twins?'' he asked uncertainly.

Whitney's eyes widened in distress. ''She didn't tell you?''

''Apparently not,'' he replied calmly. ''What didn't she tell me?''

Whitney closed her eyes. ''Oh, no,'' she groaned under her breath.

''It's all right,'' he said, the three little girls apparently sensing something and sitting quietly in his lap, staring up at him. ''Tell me.''

Whitney swallowed, then expelled a deep breath. ''My aunt won't let me stay with her if I keep the twins,'' she explained with every evidence of reluctance. ''So, Diane said I could stay with her. I—I know she called you. I guess she just never reached you. I took a nap for a while.''

He wasn't sure what he felt, but he guessed by the sudden evacuation of the triplets, and the worried look on Whitney's face, that he was emitting some negative vibrations. He struggled to remain calm and remember that Whitney was a child herself and trying to do what she thought best. Diane, as usual, was trying to be helpful and supportive. At least, he was sure that was what she was telling herself.

"Don't worry about it," he said, smiling at Whitney and the triplets who now stood around his knees uncertainly. "I was out of reach part of the time today. I'll talk to her about it tonight."

She opened her mouth as though to say something else, but the wedding party was suddenly dismissed and a stream of people started toward the door, gathering mates and children as they went, a loud and cheerful crowd on its way to the rehearsal dinner.

Jason would have caught Diane's attention, but she was in deep conversation with her father as they walked down the aisle in the wake of the rest of the family. Anger was building in him, but he did his best to keep a lid on it—primarily because he didn't entirely understand it. Was he being righteous or selfish, he wondered, because he was mad that she had made such a momentous decision without consulting him first? They'd made love and talked marriage just this morning.

He wasn't sure. He'd confront her after the dinner. Certainly he'd have it figured out by then.

CHAPTER NINE

THE WEDDING PARTY and their families filled the restaurant's small banquet room to capacity. They sat at tables of eight, eating steaks and gulf shrimp, with chicken strips and other kid-foods offered for the many children in the group. Maitland siblings and family table-hopped, enjoying the opportunity the past few weeks had provided to keep everyone in close touch.

Diane guessed she was the only one who felt left out. According to the place cards, Jason was seated beside her, but she hadn't seen him all evening. From the moment they'd arrived from the church, he'd been busy photographing the bride and groom, the toasts that preceded dinner, the food and the groups in eager conversation. He concentrated so completely on his work, that she hadn't been able to catch his eye.

And Whitney appeared to be the most de-

termined table-hopper. Her girth seemed to
have expanded considerably in the last week
and everyone seemed eager to pull up a chair
for her.

Tom and Suzanne had eyes only for their
new loves, and Diane suddenly got a feeling
from the old days—odd man out.

She excused herself though no one was
listening and headed for the ladies' room.
She was intercepted in a quiet hallway by
Jason.

Emotion leaped in her at the sight of him.
She remembered every moment of the night
before in vivid detail, and had continued to
feel his touch on her all day.

"Hi!" she said, reaching out to touch his
arm. "I've missed you! You've been so
busy all eve—" She stopped abruptly when
she noticed the thunder on his brow. As he
shifted his weight, apparently trying to keep
a considerable anger in check, she wondered
idly why she hadn't noticed it first thing. Because you're seeing him with your heart
now, a corner of her mind told her, and not
your eyes.

"Whitney's staying with you." He spoke

with a calm belied by the storm in his eyes. "And keeping her babies."

She was filled with self-recrimination. She should have made more of a point to reach him. She should have tried to talk to him before the rehearsal. She should have made sure he heard the news from her and not...whoever had told him.

"Her aunt told her..." she began to explain.

"That she can't stay with her," he cut her off, "if she keeps the babies. I know."

Then annoyance that he should be upset about that overcame her annoyance with herself. "I'm sorry that you're unhappy about that." She delivered that line with a superior tilt of her chin and the clear suggestion that he was being small to feel that way.

"I'm sorry..." he began with sudden vehemence, then lowered his voice when two waiters walked by them. "I'm sorry," he said again, "that you've found another excuse to help someone else live her life rather than have to live your own."

"What?" She demanded. That statement was like a lance through her heart. "How dare you reduce my concern for a child in dire circumstances to some…some…''

"Repressed woman's desire to live vicariously?'' he asked, pulling her aside as a man left the men's room and headed for the lounge.

She stared at him, openmouthed. "Jason!'' she finally gasped in disbelief. "She has nowhere to go! She wants to keep her babies! I can't just—''

As another group walked by, he caught her arm and led her to a door that went out to the parking lot. The night was cool, but she was flushed with anger enough not to notice. They stood under a floodlight, harshly illuminated. She noticed absently that across the parking lot, a life-size papier-mâché Santa and several reindeer took up a number of spots.

"I know,'' he said with sudden, curious calm. "You have a million noble reasons for letting her stay, and I'm the one that looks like a rat because I think you should have talked to me about it first, that you're using this as an excuse *not* to see the world you're always claiming you want to explore because deep down you're afraid of leaving home.''

"I—!" she began to deny.

He shook his head. "Like the time Suzanne broke her leg, or the time you had to get a new car. I'm sure Suzanne would have done just fine if you'd taken your trip. It's not as though she'd lost a kidney. And why in God's name would one of the wealthiest women in Texas have to choose a new car over a cruise? In that case, deciding not to touch your trust fund was an act of cowardice and not responsibility.''

Temper rose up in Diane like a geyser. She shoved Jason in the chest at that last accusation, doing it again when the first shove failed to even rock him. The second didn't, either. She was on her tiptoes with rage and frustration.

"How *dare* you accuse me of cowardice," she raged at him, "when you can't even stand still to live your life! All you've ever done is run away from it! You put on this charming vagabond front of the artist in pursuit of the perfect shot, when actually all you're doing is—is—''

She couldn't seem to decide just what it

was he was doing with his world travels. Truth be told, he'd never been entirely sure himself. But he didn't want to hear that now.

She settled down suddenly, quieting as though she'd just grasped a truth. "Are you chasing around the world, trying to find the father you've missed your whole life?" she asked.

That hit him like a hammer. Had he done that? He was always looking for the perfect shot, but was it of the ultimate foreign landscape or…the face he'd never seen?

"Or are you running away from the little life you claim you had as a child?" She got in his face, her manner pugnacious. "Afraid that if you stand still you might discover that what's lacking is in *you* and not in your life?"

That was a sucker punch. He hadn't even seen it coming. In the moment it took him to recover, he saw Diane's anger shrivel in upon itself. She looked as horrified by what she'd said as he felt.

But it was too late. The accusations were out on both sides and couldn't be taken back.

He drew a deep breath and shrugged a

shoulder, feeling as though he'd been worked over with a crowbar. But he was well aware that he'd started it. He couldn't complain.

"Then, I guess we're lucky there's going to be almost ten thousand miles between us for the next six months. If you'll excuse me." He started toward the door. Then stopped dead at the sight of Whitney holding the door open. She looked as though she'd heard everything.

He wanted to explain that he'd have had no problem with her and the babies in his life with Diane, that this quarrel was about something else entirely—but she was only sixteen, and he suddenly felt too old and weary to explain. "I'm sorry, Whitney," he said simply, and walked back into the restaurant.

IT WAS A MOMENT before Diane could pull herself together sufficiently to move. She couldn't believe that the lovemaking of last night had somehow turned into these cruel accusations and what seemed like the end of everything.

They'd talked about marriage; she should

have asked him about Whitney and the
twins. Did she go to everyone else's rescue
so that she wouldn't have to forge ahead on
her own and discover…what? That she
couldn't do it? She knew she wasn't as good
at business as her father and her siblings, but
could it be she'd find she wasn't as good at
life, either?

That was silly. She was a good teacher, a
good sister, a good friend. Wasn't that living?

Tom appeared suddenly in the doorway.
He took one look at her, pulled off his jacket
and placed it around her. "What's going
on?" he asked, guiding her toward the door.
"I saw Jason come in, grab his camera and
take off."

She told him about Whitney's aunt's decision, and her own to let Whitney stay with
her. Then she recounted her conversation
with Jason.

"You don't think you were a little hard
on him?" Tom asked gently, rubbing her
shoulders through the coat. "I mean, we've
grown up with everything. We've never felt
confined by anything. If all he knew was a
small, restricted space, why wouldn't he

want to explore the world? Why would you criticize him for that?''

"Because he criticized me," she grumbled in reply. "He called me a coward."

Tom sighed and said nothing. She looked up at him in suspicion and annoyance. "You agree with him?"

He pulled her back to him when she would have drawn away in indignation. "Not exactly. But I think you have resisted breaking free because as different as you are from Dad and Suze and me, you're your own kind of adventurer. But we've always compared you to Mom, and maybe you're afraid if you do actually take one of your fabled trips you'll no longer be our memory of her—or your own memory of her."

"But I...love Jason!" That was hard to say in view of all Jason had just said to her.

"Maybe you sabotaged your relationship deliberately to save Mom for yourself, or for all of us."

"That's ridiculous!"

"Love makes you ridiculous," he said with a philosophical smile. "Let her go, Diane. Be who *you* are. She'd have wanted that for you more than anybody. And an important detail to remember—when you're in love, home is always with you, wherever you are. Come on inside. It's about time to go home and tomorrow's going to be a killer for all of us.''

It wasn't until he opened the door that Diane remembered that Whitney had been standing there. ''Where's Whitney?'' she demanded in sudden alarm.

''Not sure,'' Tom replied. ''She told me you were out here and upset. I came right out.''

She hugged him quickly, then ran inside in pursuit of the child who had probably misinterpreted everything she'd heard tonight.

As Diane suspected, Whitney was nowhere to be found. She raced home and noticed the car with the Texas state seal on the door parked in front of her building. ''Oh, no!'' she groaned under her breath as she went up in the elevator, then let herself into the apartment.

She heard conversation coming from Whitney's room and hurried in to find Whitney packing, Anita Sanchez, her caseworker, helping her. Anita was short and slender, a lot of concern and resourcefulness packed into her tiny body. Diane had come to know Anita fairly well since taking in Whitney.

"What's happening?" Diane asked.

"Anita's found me a great place to live," Whitney said, a smile in place, though it didn't show at all in her eyes. "You don't have to worry about me anymore."

"We've had a vacancy open up at Haven House," Anita explained, coming to put an arm around Diane. "One of the girls went home. Don't look so upset. This is a responsibility you shouldn't have had in the first place."

Diane appreciated Anita's concern, but had to set her straight. "It was a responsibility I gladly undertook."

"But your situation's changed now," Anita said. "And that's all right. You're allowed to—"

"Anita, please," Diane interrupted. "I want—"

"I heard you and Jason arguing," Whitney said without condemnation. "He's such a sweetie. I don't want the two of you to break up because of me."

"We didn't break up because of you,"

Diane corrected forcefully. "But because we...I..."

"Because you didn't ask him if I could stay with you. I understand that. You were going to meet him in...wherever that was...on spring break, and you wouldn't be able to do that if I've just delivered."

"Whitney, it wasn't that Jason didn't want you living with us. It was—"

"I know," Whitney interrupted. "It was that you hadn't asked him first. But if I stay, you'll always be worrying about me instead of worrying about him, and that isn't right. People in love are supposed to think about each other."

"I'm the caseworker here," Anita said, getting between them. "May I say something?"

"No." A new voice—distinctly male— turned all three women toward the bedroom door. Jason stood in the opening still wearing the suit he'd worn to dinner and looking exhausted but determined. "As the party whose motives are in question here, I think I should get to speak."

"You don't have to explain—" Whitney began.

"I think I do," he insisted, indicating the half-packed suitcase. "Judging by the fact that you seem to think you're going somewhere."

"Anita's found me a place at Haven House," Whitney said.

"Haven House?"

"It's a home for unwed teens," Anita replied.

Jason turned his attention to her and offered his hand. "I'm Jason Morris," he said. "Diane's fiancé."

Anita took it. "Anita Sanchez. Whitney's caseworker. She called me here, thinking she should change residences."

"She's mistaken. My quarrel with Diane was that I'd been left out of the decision, not that she'd made it. I'm fond of Whitney, too, and if she wants to keep the twins, I think that's fine." He turned to Diane with a look she couldn't read.

Diane felt hopeful, confused and overwhelmed. "I'm not entirely sure what you're saying," Diane admitted.

Jason ran a hand over his face, then asked the caseworker politely, "Would you excuse

Diane and Whitney and me for a few minutes, please?''

Anita narrowed her eyes on him for a moment, then asked Whitney, ''Is that all right with you?''

''Yes,'' Whitney assured her quickly. ''He's a very nice man.''

''Then I'll be in the living room,'' Anita said, and left the room, closing the door behind her.

''Do you want to stay with Diane?'' Jason asked Whitney candidly.

She frowned and looked away. ''Not if it interferes…''

''It doesn't.''

''You were fighting.''

''We were discussing,'' he corrected.

''You broke up!''

''No, we didn't.'' He turned to Diane with a look that challenged her to dispute that. She glared back at him, but didn't try to argue. ''Being this close requires a lot more give and take than either of us is used to doing so far. Me, particularly. It's going to take a little time to perfect it. Do you want to stay?''

Whitney folded her arms atop the mound of her tummy. "Yes, I do."

"Then, you will." He opened the door and smiled apologetically. "But for the moment, could you go sit with Anita and give us a few minutes alone?"

She walked off with a bright smile, and Jason closed the door again.

"Now, for you," he said to Diane.

CHAPTER TEN

DIANE LOOKED UNCERTAIN but still quarrelsome as she stood on the other side of the bed from him. He knew he had to get her on his side if he was going to make her understand his position.

"I'm sorry," he said without preamble. "I think my anger was justified, but not my attack. I know that kindness and concern guide your actions with everyone."

She stared at him in surprise, apparently speechless. She cleared her throat, opened her mouth to speak, but nothing came out.

So he kept talking. "If Whitney's going to stay with you and keep her babies," he said, "then you're going to need help."

"Suzanne said she'd—"

"I mean live-in help."

He could see in her eyes that she guessed his meaning, but wasn't certain.

"You're going to be in Nouméa."

He shook his head. "I just woke up my agent and told him I was sending the check back to my publisher, and suggested a photographer I thought would do good work for them."

She blinked at him. He really liked having her off balance—even if only for a few seconds.

"You...*what?*"

He had the edge now. He took a few steps toward her, trying not to swagger. "I sent the check back. I'm staying." He grinned. "And I'm now completely dependent upon your support and Anna's good will in finding me more work."

She looked thrilled for the space of several heartbeats, then her smile folded and she whispered earnestly, "You'll hate me if you do this."

He was able to smile in the face of that threat. "Diane, I love you so much, I could sacrifice my life, never mind my book contract. I was wrong about your motives for staying home, but you were right about mine for chasing around the world. I was looking for something, but it wasn't my father. And I realized when I was driving around aimlessly tonight, seeing Christmas lights and happy groups, that it was time I stopped thinking about what I'd missed and concentrate on what I have.'' This question was tough. "If I still have it?''

That earned him just the reaction he'd hoped for. She flung herself at him and he caught her, feeling her tears on his cheek, her leg wrapping itself around his hip for stability.

He'd been right. This was it. He had his arms full of the love he'd been searching for.

"No!'' she said firmly, scaring him into putting her down. His throat went dry and his heart slapped against his ribs.

"You can't give up your life's dream for me,'' she said, her small hands pinching his forearms in a sturdy grip. "I won't let you. We'll get married, you'll go to Nouméa, and I'll come to you in the summer when—''

He shook his head. "You don't run this relationship, remember?'' he reminded quietly. "We do it together. There'll be other contracts, other opportunities to travel. But right now, this is where we both need to be.''

Her mouth trembled and her face began to crumple. "Are you sure?"

"Absolutely."

"You were right about why I stay home," she said, standing away from him as though offering a confession. "Tom agrees with you. He says I'm really afraid to go. That I'm afraid I'll lose the part of me that's my mother if I do."

"You're tougher than that," he reassured her, surprised that she saw herself as an extension of her mother. "You handle all the emotional, generous sorts of things that everyone else is reluctant to give. You don't borrow that from her. That's you." He framed her face in his hands and kissed her. "Except in my case, where I'm sort of getting your insights by osmosis or kissing, or something."

She smiled at him, clearly delighted that he thought they still shared things. The look in her eyes, he thought, would sustain him for a lifetime.

He heard Anita rap on the door. "Everything all right in there?" He heard it squeak open as Diane kissed him senseless. "Oh, well, yeah!'' he heard Anita say as Whitney giggled. "I guess it is."

THE WEDDING WAS a beautiful affair with the bride in an ivory suit, all her daughters, daughters-in-law, and stepdaughters attending her in knee-length dresses of emerald taffeta.

The groom wore a dark suit, his son serving as best man, his stepsons and in-laws making up a handsome line of groomsmen.

The church was filled to capacity. There were poinsettias everywhere, fat garlands wrapped with pearls decorating the altar and cordoning off the family pews.

There were so many well-wishers that it took an eternity for the wedding party to get to the reception. Diane was able only to wave at Jason as he slaved over his camera, and smile at Whitney, who looked beautiful if a little pale in a yellow wool dress that made her hair look like a flame.

Diane noticed that Elliott Brody, a classmate of Whitney's, and the grandson of a friend of Megan's, took her arm to help her down the church steps, and said something that made her laugh. He was a student Diane liked particularly because he was always attentive and interested.

Today Diane felt as though she were living someone else's miracle. Her father was ecstatically happy with Megan, her siblings had each found love, and she... There were no words to describe the warmth and hope that filled her, the sweetness of her life at the moment.

She spotted Tom and Claire in their wedding finery, happily arm in arm. Then she saw them look into one another's eyes and share a moment of bitter disappointment. She knew they were thinking of Whitney's twins. Then they held each other for a moment, linked hands and moved on.

They'd find another baby, Tom had assured Diane. She hoped it was soon.

Diane turned to make sure Whitney had a ride to the reception and saw her standing by herself, watching Tom and Claire walk away, her own features grim. Then Elliott caught her arm and helped her down the steps to an old red pickup.

The buffet was sumptuous, and the room looked beautiful. Guests filled the tables, stood around in knots of conversation in the middle of the room, and wandered around its edges, reading the maps, searching for spots of interest and finding them.

Megan came to hug Diane. ''I have the most brilliant and wonderful group of children a mother could hope to produce, and yet you and Tom and Suzanne add another level of artistry to the mix that stuns me. I hope you're just a fraction as happy to have me join your family as I am to have you in mine.''

Diane clutched her hands. ''I'm thrilled, Megan. I've been a long time without a mother.''

Megan hugged her again. ''Promise you'll come to me if you need anything.'' She grinned. ''Your father tells me you and Jason are getting married.''

''Yes, we are. There isn't going to be a Blake left unmarried by February.''

Strong arms wrapped around Diane from behind.

''Smart girl,'' her father said, kissing her cheek. ''I do like that boy. When he was photographing us earlier, I asked him when he was leaving, and he told me he's staying with you and Whitney. But what about the book deal?"

Diane was still amazed by that. "He returned the advance," she replied.

Hugh and Megan looked astonished. "That's the kind of love that couldn't be shouted any louder in a ten-karat diamond," her father said.

"Miss Blake!"

Elliott suddenly appeared at Megan's elbow, his pale anxious face looking desperately into Diane's.

Hugh dropped his arms from her and she stiffened. "What is it?"

"Whitney doesn't feel well." He pointed toward the large double doors that led to the hallway. "I think she's having the babies."

Diane excused herself to her father and Megan, and ran toward the doors. Elliott kept abreast of her.

At the doors, he pointed her toward the corridor that led to the ladies' room. "She said something about her water something and went in there. I got Dr. McDermott."

Diane burst into the outer lounge to find Abby and Claire had already stripped Whitney of the probably ruined yellow dress and wrapped her in a man's raincoat.

Whitney was pale and breathing a little hard, though she seemed relatively calm. She reached for Diane's hand. "They're even earlier than Abby thought," she said as Claire belted the raincoat while Abby used a cell phone to tell Maitland Maternity they were on their way. "But Claire says they have every chance of being okay."

"She should know." Diane squeezed Whitney's hand. "I didn't bring my own car. I rode with Suzanne and Doug so I didn't have to ride in Jason's open Jeep in this." She held out the skirt of her bridesmaid's dress.

"Tom's already pulling our car around the back," Claire said. She and Abby were in professional mode, smiling but serious as they bustled Whitney out into the hallway.

Tom was loping up the corridor, his car idling by the open rear exit doors.

"I'll see you at the hospital!" Elliott shouted at her as she was led toward the exit, Tom and Claire on either side of her, Abby offering instructions.

Diane followed, feeling required to wave her off before finding Jason.

But he was already in the parking lot with a crowd of guests who'd heard the news from Megan and Hugh and appeared to give Whitney a rousing send-off. He photographed her surprised smile and wave at the crowd, then Abby and Claire following her into the car.

The moment the car sped away, Megan came to take Jason's camera. "Go to the hospital. We've got enough pictures."

"It's your wedding," Diane said reasonably. "These are once-in-a-lifetime shots. I'll go to the hospital, and Jason can stay and—"

Hugh turned to Jason. "Will you please get her out of here? She's always trying to make everything work out perfectly for everyone, instead of doing what's best for herself. Go. Be with Whitney."

Jason caught Diane's hand and ran for the Jeep.

Tom sat with Jason in the waiting room. "I'm glad Whitney asked Claire to stay with her and Diane," he said. "Claire's very good at what she does. Even I was amazed at how well she's handled all this, considering the stake we once had in the babies. But she wants their safety before any personal considerations.''

Jason understood his amazement. Diane was continually confounding him. ''Women generally astound me. My mother lived kind of a small life, but every moment of it was for me. I've seen it all over the world—women who bear enormous loads and unthinkable hardships just to raise their children to healthy adulthood. Then I met Diane, who put her own life second to the needs of a student she cared about. I don't know many guys who'd do that.''

''No.'' Tom stretched and groaned. ''I wonder how much longer.''

Jason was happy to be relegated to a waiting room. Birthing rooms where everyone made a party out of childbirth had never appealed to him—not that he'd ever had the opportunity to weigh in with an opinion before.

''I'm glad we can wait out here. Though those babies don't have a father here, they certainly have enough people praying for their safety and good health.''

''Whitney has a lot of friends at school,'' Elliott said. He'd been waiting with them since shortly after they'd arrived. ''They were hoping she'd have the first baby of the year so she could get all the gifts they give.''

''You must be a particularly good friend,'' Jason observed.

Elliott shrugged. ''She was nice to me. When we first moved here, none of the kids would talk to me because my family was rich. They thought I'd be stuck-up or something. But she always talked to me. Because she never had any money, she knew what it was like to be a minority.'' He nodded thoughtfully. ''It isn't just the color of skin that makes minorities, you know.''

Tom met Jason's eye. That was a profound observation for a kid. He had possibilities.

Tom downed the end of a cup of vending machine coffee. They'd been waiting almost five hours.

''Diane told me you're filing for adoption with the state,'' Jason said.

Tom nodded. ''We're both anxious to get

a family under way." He smiled sympathetically at Jason. "You're going to have a
teenager and babies keeping you up nights
before you're even adjusted to being married."

Jason laughed. "Life's never what you
expect, is it?"

"No, it isn't."

The waiting room door burst open suddenly and Diane appeared, weary face
wreathed in smiles. "We have two beautiful,
very healthy, fraternal twin boys. No
breathing problems. No problems at all!
Come and see!"

Elliott got to his feet, but stood there uncertainly. Diane beckoned him to join them.

BEAUTIFUL, Jason decided, was a very sub-
jective opinion. The two babies in Whitney's
arms were very red, a little squashed looking, and with their tiny little mouths puck-
ered, tongues moving in and out, bearing a
remarkable resemblance to a pair of fish.

But when he looked at them with the
knowledge that they would live in his home
and, for a time, at least, be a part of his

family, he had to admit that he considered them beautiful, too.

Whitney was pale and tired, but curiously serene. She looked at one baby, then the other, then up at Diane, as though amazed by what she'd produced. Diane leaned down to rest her cheek against Whitney's hair. "Well done, sweetie." she said.

"I DIDN'T KNOW you were here, Elliott," Whitney said, looking pleasantly surprised to see him.

"They have long fingers," Elliott said, pointing his own index toward the tiny hand of the closest baby. "Definitely football team draft picks. Can you have a vanilla milkshake?"

He looked at their companions. "That's her favorite thing."

"I think I can eat whatever I want."

"Lone Star's still open. I'll be right back." He touched her arm wrapped around the baby in an artlessly affectionate way.

Her eyes followed him to the door. "Thanks, Elliott."

"Now, there's a good friend," Claire

said. "What are you going to name the babies, Whitney?"

Jason saw a ripple of emotion cross Whitney's face. It was pain so enormous that for a moment he thought she would cry out, or make some urgent, physical complaint.

But instead, she said to Claire, "Here, Claire. Would you hold one?"

"I'd love to." Claire reached down to scoop up the nearest baby, her face aglow with happiness over the safe delivery.

"Tom?" Whitney held the second baby toward him.

He looked reluctant.

Diane bent his arm for him, took the baby and placed him in it. "See? Nothing to it. If you're going to find your own babies some day, you should—"

"These are their babies," Whitney said, that pained look gone from her face as she seemed to square her shoulders against the pillows and make herself smile. "You and Tom should name them, Claire."

Everyone froze. Claire and Tom, arms filled with babies, looked at one another in confusion.

"I wanted so much to be their mother,"

Whitney said, swallowing with apparent difficulty, "but I've learned a lot about love over the past couple of weeks. Diane changed her life to help me, Jason traded in his dream to stay with her because he knew she needed him, and the two of you have done so much to help me even though I've disappointed you." She heaved a deep sigh, and smiled, seemingly strengthened somehow by that admission. "You've all done so much to give me the best possible chance to have what I want, so I think the best chance I can give my babies to have what I want for them, is to give them to you." Her eyes welled with tears but she continued to smile as she looked from Claire to Tom. "If you still want that."

Though he had no camera, Jason knew that moment was forever imprinted in his mind, on his heart.

Tom put his free arm around Claire as she dissolved into happy sobs, the babies sleeping soundly, unaware at the moment of how generous their mother was.

Diane, dark eyes streaming tears, wrapped Whitney in her arms. "I know how hard this is, Whitney,'' she said. ''But it's right. I'm sure it's right.''

''I know it is.'' Whitney insisted, but she sobbed all the same.

A nurse came to reclaim the babies for a few more tests, and Tom and Claire relinquished them with obvious reluctance.

''You're sure, Whitney?'' Claire asked as the nurse disappeared.

Finally composed, Whitney nodded. ''Yes, I am.''

''Maybe I should leave the three of you to talk things over,'' Diane said, swiping at her eyes with a tissue. She caught Jason by the hand and dragged him out of the room behind her. Once in the hall, she collapsed in tears against him.

He pulled her toward the empty waiting room and sat her down. ''She's doing the right thing,'' he said. ''You know she is.''

She nodded. ''But I've been with her through it all, and I know what this is costing her.''

''But she's big enough to do it. Now she'll be invincible her whole life long.''

Diane quieted and leaned into him. ''What do we do now?''

Jason leaned back in the uncomfortable vinyl sofa and held her close. "Well, I guess we get her through high school, send her off to college and travel when we can work it in."

She couldn't quite believe her ears. She sat up to look into his face, thinking that for someone who claimed to be newly exposed to the giving emotions, he was learning fast.

"Her aunt said Whitney could live with her if—"

He kissed her forehead. "But Whitney would prefer to stay with you, and you'd like that, too."

She felt the warmth of his body under her fingertips, the warmth of his heart in her own. "But that's a lot to ask of you."

"Love is a lot to ask of anyone, but it turns the world, and if you don't have it, or can't give it, you're just not equipped to be here. And you're definitely not a Blake or a Maitland."

She kissed him soundly, wrapped her arms around him and squeezed as hard as she could. She was too happy to contain all the strength love gave her. "Or a Morris!" she said.

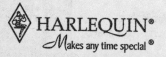

Harlequin Historicals®
invites you
to ring in the holidays with

'Tis the Season

This festive anthology from three of your
favorite authors features these dazzling tales
set during the holiday season:

"A Promise To Keep" by Susan Spencer Paul
A tender Regency romance in which Garan Baldwin
gallantly rescues the woman he's determined to marry
when he discovers her stranded during a snowstorm!

"Christmas at Wayfarer Inn" by Shari Anton
Passion ignites in this delightful medieval tale when a
dashing nobleman claims the heart of a beautiful innkeeper....

"Twelfth Knight" by Tori Phillips
In this seventh installment of Tori Phillips's
popular British Tudor miniseries—
the Cavendish Chronicles—a disguised knight accepts
a challenge to woo the tempestuous Lady Alyssa!

'TIS THE SEASON
AVAILABLE IN STORES NOVEMBER 2001!

Harlequin Historicals®
Historical Romantic Adventure!

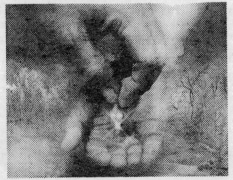

Together for the first time
in one Collector's Edition!

New York Times bestselling authors

Barbara Delinsky

Catherine Coulter   Linda Howard

Forever Yours

A special trade-size volume containing three
complete novels that showcase the passion,
imagination and stunning power that these
talented authors are famous for.

Coming to your favorite retail outlet in December 2001.